"Let me have him. I want to make his last hours on this earth as hard on him as he has made it on the poor girls he preyed upon."

"What if I say no?"

"Who is he to you?" She glared at him in defiance.

Slocum had no answer for her. He swept the man's handgun off the ground and took two knives from the scabbards on him.

"Senõr, Mother of God. Please don't leave me with her," Castro begged.

"I think when you chose to ride with Cicatrize, you never expected to fall in such hands. But I am out-voted in this camp by angry women. Where are your horses?" He looked around in the night for them.

"You can't!" His desperate plea shattered the air.

"I'll find them," he said, more to himself than to the fear-stricken outlaw or her, and started uphill to look for them. He shut his ears to Castro's cries and began to climb the slope for the timber. They'd be tethered up there somewhere.

In a short while he found the two hip-shot horses. Castro's cries reverberated off of the towering ranges.

DON'T MISS THESE
ALL-ACTION WESTERN SERIES
FROM THE BERKLEY PUBLISHING GROUP

THE GUNSMITH by J. R. Roberts
Clint Adams was a legend among lawmen, outlaws, and ladies. They called him . . . the Gunsmith.

LONGARM by Tabor Evans
The popular long-running series about Deputy U.S. Marshal Long—his life, his loves, his fight for justice.

SLOCUM by Jake Logan
Today's longest-running action Western. John Slocum rides a deadly trail of hot blood and cold steel.

BUSHWHACKERS by B. J. Lanagan
An action-packed series by the creators of Longarm! The rousing adventures of the most brutal gang of cutthroats ever assembled—Quantrill's Raiders.

DIAMONDBACK by Guy Brewer
Dex Yancey is Diamondback, a Southern gentleman turned con man when his brother cheats him out of the family fortune. Ladies love him. Gamblers hate him. But nobody pulls one over on Dex . . .

WILDGUN by Jack Hanson
The blazing adventures of mountain man Will Barlow—from the creators of Longarm!

TEXAS TRACKER by Tom Calhoun
Meet J.T. Law: the most relentless—and dangerous—manhunter in all Texas. Where sheriffs and posses fail, he's the best man to bring in the most vicious outlaws—for a price.

JAKE LOGAN

SLOCUM AND THE SIERRA MADRAS GOLD

J

JOVE BOOKS, NEW YORK

THE BERKLEY PUBLISHING GROUP
Published by the Penguin Group
Penguin Group (USA) Inc.
375 Hudson Street, New York, New York 10014, USA
Penguin Group (Canada), 10 Alcorn Avenue, Toronto, Ontario M4V 3B2, Canada
(a division of Pearson Penguin Canada Inc.)
Penguin Books Ltd., 80 Strand, London WC2R 0RL, England
Penguin Group Ireland, 25 St. Stephen's Green, Dublin 2, Ireland (a division of Penguin Books Ltd.)
Penguin Group (Australia), 250 Camberwell Road, Camberwell, Victoria 3124, Australia
(a division of Pearson Australia Group Pty. Ltd.)
Penguin Books India Pvt. Ltd., 11 Community Centre, Panchsheel Park, New Delhi—110 017, India
Penguin Group (NZ), Cnr. Airborne and Rosedale Roads, Albany, Auckland 1310, New Zealand
(a division of Pearson New Zealand Ltd.)
Penguin Books (South Africa) (Pty.) Ltd., 24 Sturdee Avenue, Rosebank, Johannesburg 2196,
South Africa

Penguin Books Ltd., Registered Offices: 80 Strand, London WC2R 0RL, England

This is a work of fiction. Names, characters, places, and incidents either are the product of the author's imagination or are used fictitiously, and any resemblance to actual persons, living or dead, business establishments, events, or locales is entirely coincidental.

SLOCUM AND THE SIERRA MADRAS GOLD

A Jove Book / published by arrangement with the author

PRINTING HISTORY
Jove edition / July 2005

Copyright © 2005 by The Berkley Publishing Group.

ISBN: 0-515-13965-3

JOVE®
Jove Books are published by The Berkley Publishing Group,
a division of Penguin Group (USA) Inc.,
375 Hudson Street, New York, New York 10014.
JOVE is a registered trademark of Penguin Group (USA) Inc.
The "J" design is a trademark belonging to Penguin Group (USA) Inc.

PRINTED IN THE UNITED STATES OF AMERICA

10 9 8 7 6 5 4 3 2 1

1

Somewhere off in the azure sky and craggy peaks above him, a gliding harpy eagle shrieked at the invasion of his domain. The bird's shrill cry drew a smile to the corners of Slocum's sun-blistered lips. He must be close to the refuge he sought in the small village of Sierra Estria. The dun horse's shoes clicked on the narrow road's rocky surface that wound skyward. Hardly more than a two-wheel *caretia* path, most supplies to this remote place came in via pack trains of burros.

Close by, the silver stream gurgled and rushed over centuries of worn, smooth rocks. The musical wind in the ponderosa boughs and the water's song along with a chorus of the noisy jaybirds, camprobbers and magpies made a symphony. What filled his ears was the song of the Sierra Madras and he daydreamed of the days ahead. Swivel-hipped young *putas* dancing to a fast Spanish guitar in the tree-filtered sunshine on the patio beside a cantina. The noisy clacks of their castanets in accompaniment, and their provocative movements tempted their onlookers to seek the supple bodies under the thin cloth of their skirts and low-cut blouses.

He wet his cracked lips in anticipation of squeezing

such firm flesh. Deep in his thoughts of pleasure, he let the head-swinging dun clack its way around the twists of mountain road in its smooth-running walk. Then he saw someone lying in the trail and reined up the gelding. His right hand sought the butt of his Colt. Closing his fingers on the satin-smooth redwood handles, he searched about in the trees and boulders on the steep slope above and beneath him. Nothing looked out of place.

Every muscle in his body tensed as he stepped down; the dun with its head down snorted wearily in the dust. Who was this person? He was hatless and dressed in the clothes of a gringo. No gunbelt, the dark stains in the back of the tan shirt were no doubt blood. With caution, Logan knelt beside him and turned the man over. His shirtfront was crimson with blood that had mixed with the fine dust, making red mud that clung to the material.

The man's eyes flickered deep in some far-off existence and a weak voice spoke, "They took the gold—but there's more. The map—" He coughed and used up more of his meager strength. "Linda . . . Mercado . . . she has it for me."

The man's look began to dissolve in and out of the living. Slocum knew he was too late to save the fast-fading life, but he wondered if he knew his killers.

"Who did this to you?"

The man looked downward with effort and opened the right fist at his side. A shiny concha button sat in the middle of his calloused palm. Slocum nodded, and the light behind the victim's brown eyes went out. He closed the lids, made a quick examination of the hammered coin, pocketed it and went for his ground cloth. There was a padre at Estria that would see that the man was properly buried.

The body wrapped and across the saddle in front of him, Slocum resumed his ride on to the village. Somehow the discovery of the victim had taken some of the fandango spirit away from him. Soon he reached the long valley lined with small farms that watered their crops and orchards from the creek. The green of alfalfa and its pungent aroma when mowed filled the air. Ripe peaches and golden apricots hung on the trees. Frijoles and black bean bushes were laid out in uniform rows and the tasseled corn rustled in the soft wind.

A dead man with a secret about gold lay over his lap. No ID on him, no name to give him—perhaps in Estria they would know him and the woman who had hidden his map. He crossed the arched bridge built of stones and clattered up the rocks set like bricks in the street.

He paused before the cantina, dismounted heavily and looked at the faded black sign on the stucco wall. PALACIA REALE. The King's Place, he translated and smiled. Hardly what he considered the king's anything, but no matter. He pushed through the swinging green doors and into the shadowy darkness of the interior. A strong smell of tobacco, the sourness of beer and cheap perfume filled his nose. The smile on the bartender's face and his straight, white teeth glistened in the subdued light.

"Hello, amigo."

Slocum nodded. "Come outside here. There is a dead man I found on the road today. I need to know his name."

"Me?" The man blanched even in the dim light, setting down the glass he polished.

"You got a twin?"

"No, señor, but I don't like to look at dead people."

"It won't take long."

The man glanced around as if to find help for his situation, but no one was in the barroom and, at last, he agreed with a nod to join Slocum, who held his hand out toward the doorway.

Outside, Slocum unleashed the ropes and exposed the man's dusty brown hair. With a fist full of it, he raised the blanched body faceup.

The bartender swallowed hard and his dark eyes flew

wide open. "That—that is Señor Ray." His view of the corpse had no doubt shaken him.

"Ray who?" Slocum recovered the dead man.

"Martin Ray."

"He lives here?"

"No—"

"But you knew him?"

The man managed to nod, swallowed hard again and looked ready to flee.

"He came to Estria every few months. He was miner, señor."

"Where at?"

The bartender turned up his palms and shook his head. "I have no idea."

"No kinfolk here?"

"No, señor. May I go back inside?"

"Sure," Slocum agreed. Obviously, the man was nervous as a long-tail cat in a room full of rockers around the dead man.

The bartender disappeared inside the green doors of the cantina. Slocum shoved his felt hat up on his head with his thumb and studied the small chapel built of rock and mortar with the bell tower. He better go over there and find the padre. After he got Ray put in the ground, there would be plenty of time to go find this Linda. His responsibility for the moment was to get the corpse off his horse. Someone would need to dig the grave, and by then he would have found and notified her about his demise—if she was about the small village.

"What's on your horse?" a small, barefoot boy in ragged shorts asked in Spanish, braver than the others standing back like a small troop in the shadows.

"A dead man," Slocum said, leading the dun toward the church.

"Did you shoot him?" he asked, tagging along.

"No, some *banditos* did."

"Did you shoot them?" The boy bravely smiled back at his friends as if to brag on his own boldness for asking this gringo such strong questions.

"You writing a book?" Slocum asked, wrapping the reins on the hitch rail at the church's stoop.

"No, but I wanted to know."

"I never saw the killers. Good enough?"

"Who will bury him?"

"I hope the padre."

The boy followed him, a few steps behind, and Slocum pushed one of the great wooden doors open, looking at the benchless interior. Many of the churches had no pews, the congregation either knelt or stood for the services. He removed his hat and stepped inside the sanctuary. Flickering candles on the altar cast an eerie light on the crucifixion statue above them.

"May I help you?" A priest appeared at the side doorway and bowed his head at the altar, then moved in his long robes toward Slocum.

"My name's Slocum. I found a dead man on the road. His name is Ray, according to the bartender at the Palacia Reale, and Ray has no relatives here. He was robbed and has no money on him—but I would pay for his grave to be dug."

"I am Father Cedillo. That would be very generous of you, señor."

"How much will that be?"

"Ten pesos for services and all?"

"Fine." Slocum dug the money from his vest and paid him. "There is a woman here who knew him—Linda Mercado."

"Yes, I know her." Father Cedillo was a man in his forties and balding on top. He nodded.

"I would go and tell her if you'd like. Where might I find her?"

"She has a *jacal* up the hill from the Reale. The fourth one on the left."

"Fine, can I assist you in bringing in the body?"

"No, I will get the gardener Jose to help me. We will come out front."

Slocum nodded.

Outside, his fingers combed back the too-long hair, then he replaced his hat. The half dozen, wide-eyed youths were standing at a safe enough distance when their spokesman came forward.

"They taking him?"

Slocum nodded, undoing the rope over the horn that kept his horse in place. "Yeah, they said they had plenty of room for three or four more."

The youth squinted his eyes. "What do you mean?"

"They have several graves for over-curious boys that ask too many questions."

The others laughed at his put-down. Their spokesman scowled at Slocum's humor and started to walk away.

"Wait! What color horse did this gringo ride out of here on?"

The boy twisted and squinted hard at him. "What do you pay?"

Slocum dug out a ten *centavo* piece and flipped it toward him. "What color?"

The youth caught the coin in the air, but not without a quick glance at it to be sure it was real. He looked up hard at Slocum. "A bald-face sorrel horse with a *quatro* branded on his right shoulder."

"Good enough." A bald-faced horse with a five brand on his right shoulder wouldn't be hard to recognize, if he ever spotted it.

"This is Jose, Señor Slocum" the padre said, introducing the short man to Slocum.

"Good to meet you," Slocum said and helped the two unload the body. They soon assured him they could handle it and went through the gate into the courtyard with their burden.

Slocum swung into the saddle. One more chore—go find this Linda and tell her. Maybe she still had Ray's map.

"You need anything else, my name is Ruel," the boy said, hurrying alongside his stirrup.

"For now, I know enough."

"Be careful, gringo."

Slocum nodded that he'd heard his warning. He wondered if he should have asked his informant if he knew who had killed Ray. That could wait for later.

The dusty pathway up the hillside from the cantina was steep. He passed several hovels with barking dogs and wide-eyed children looking with frowns at the invader. He dismounted at the fourth home and hitched the dun to the dusty juniper bush. Tufts of dried grass dotted the ground and the door was open. He stopped at the wooden framework.

"Anyone home?"

"Who is there?" a sleep-choked voice asked.

"My name's Slocum."

Still half asleep, a woman appeared wrapped in a black cotton blanket that she held closed with one hand, as the second one tossed her dark hair aside from her face. With her high cheekbones, she looked part Indian, but the starkness of the rest held a haughty look that wasn't that at all. Perhaps five feet tall, she looked slender under the trailing blanket.

"What can I do for you?"

"There was a man named Ray who knew you?"

"Yes, he was here only last night." Her left eyelid flickered as she looked with sharp concern at him.

"Bandits killed him on the road."

"Oh, no," she cried and fell into his arms. He felt her trembling as he held her tight. The sobs shook her entire body as she wept. Ray at least had someone to cry over his death.

2

They stood in the coolness after the late afternoon thunder-storm that sent icy droplets from the sky, and blinding bolts of lightning with thunder roared through the peaks of the mother mountains. Slocum was with Linda and three of her girlfriends, all dressed in black, and the street boy Ruel, at the graveside. The padre gave the words in Latin and waved the smoky container over the corpse still wrapped in his canvas ground cloth. The girls crossed themselves and genuflected at the end.

"Good day and may God be with you, my children," Cedillo said to them and they nodded in approval at him, herding the sobbing Linda from the fenced-in graveyard.

The walk was long back to her place. The others shook their heads, occasionally at Slocum, over her condition. He nodded in agreement as the black-dressed entourage made its way over the uneven rock outcroppings that showed up in the street. At last, they began the march uphill to Linda's *jacal* and the boy Ruel stopped.

"I will see you, señor," he said.

Slocum halted and let the foursome get a ways ahead.

"Do you know who shot him?" Slocum asked the boy quietly.

8

"No, señor."

Slocum looked to a far-off peak that glistened red in the sundown. "Could you guess, who did it?"

"When I can, I will find you."

"Good enough, Ruel. But don't let the killers know a thing or it might be your life."

"I savvy that, señor."

Slocum nodded in approval and hurried to catch up with the women.

When he reached the *jacal*, he found they had put the brokenhearted Linda to bed in a hammock in the side shed. They rushed about with their veils swept up, making some food. One of the girls patted out flour tortillas in her hands while resting on her knees. Another built the fire up with small pieces of split mountain oak. The third, with her sleeves rolled up, was busy chopping cilantro.

"Linda is taking his death very hard," Mucho said, looking around for a place to put the first tortilla. The girl, like the others, was in her late teens. Mucho showed her Mestiza blood in the full lips and large eyes.

The fire builder was slender, and moved catlike. Her eyes were shaped like an Asian in the corners; he decided she was part Apache or Yaqui. High cheekbones and dark bow lips; her skin was darker than the others—they called her Tuey.

Chopping the cilantro was the thicker set one of the girls. With a soggy body, she had the biggest breasts, the ample waist, but still in girl-like proportions that made her appealing enough to any man, Slocum decided. They called her Pearl.

"What is your business here?" Mucho asked him, finishing another tortilla and testing the griddle with her mouth-wetted fingertip. Satisfied, she tossed the white circle on the iron.

Slocum squatted on his boot heels with his back to the wall. "I wanted to get away and have some time to think."

The Indian one, Tuey, laughed aloud. "All of us wish for the day we have enough money to leave this place and you come here."

"There are much worse places than Estria," he said as Pearl brought him some red wine in a cup. He toasted her and said thanks.

"But where is that, in hell?" Mucho asked.

"You girls are not slaves here, are you?"

"No!"

"In Mexico City, you would be. Same in Juarez."

"But I want a fine house, a husband and children," Mucho said, tossing the tortilla over with her fingers.

"Do you really?" Slocum asked.

"Of course I do."

"But then you could not flirt with every man. He would get angry and then you could not get drunk, he would get mad."

"Ah, I see what he means," Pearl said. "You see some guy you think would be a *mucho grande* and you'd have to sit cross-legged all night." She laughed aloud at her own joke and then covered her mouth with her hand as if embarrassed by her outburst.

"If we don't feed this hombre soon," Tuey said, "he may be too weak to even lay one of us."

Slocum heard their words and about agreed with them. Food would be nice. He hadn't eaten since some dried jerky early that morning.

"Who killed Ray?" he asked, hearing horses pulling up in front of the *jacal* and the neighbors dogs raising Cain.

Tuey rushed to the doorway and turned back with a frown at the others.

"Ah, they said all the town's *putas* are up here!" someone with a rasping voice shouted outside.

"Go home!" Tuey shouted from the doorway. "We are having a wake," she said, holding a finger to her mouth to quiet them. "Hush up, go home."

A man's voice laughed out loud. "Why hell, honey, I've got a hard-on big as an elephant—"

"Go home," Tuey repeated. "Linda's friend was shot today and he barely lies in his grave."

Slocum's ear turned to hear them. He rose to his feet and his hand went to his gun butt—not knowing what to expect. Pearl crossed over to him and held his forearm for a moment.

"They will leave," she said and dismissed his concern with a shake of her head.

"Who died, by the way?" the one outside asked.

"The gringo named Ray."

"Shitfire, who would miss him?"

In the doorway, Tuey stood shaking her head in disapproval, but the men outside must have been mounting up. Slocum could hear the sounds of it—still he wanted a look at them. No confrontation, but who were they and what was their business? The lack of a window in the wall stopped that. At the sounds of their leaving, he nodded at Pearl in approval, and squatted back down to sip his wine and watch the tortilla-making process.

Mucho dug some frijoles out of a pot on the fire to place in the center of the flour wrap, sprinkled some cilantro on them, folded it up and handed it to him.

"I hope they are hot enough," she said.

"Who was out there?" he asked, giving her a nod of thanks for the food.

"Juarez Vargas and his men."

"What do they do?"

Mucho shrugged her thin shoulders underneath the ruffles of the black dress. "Bandits, soldiers of fortune, no?"

"They rob Ray?"

"Maybe; who would know?" She busied herself making more tortillas for the others.

The four of them sat around eating as twilight darkened the house until only the glow of the fireplace was casting their huge shadows on the wall. They spoke of small things and laughed about Tuey telling of a man who came rushing into her shack in the daytime, undressing as fast as he could and when he was naked looking down and seeing his manhood had gone limp.

"What then?" Pearl asked her.

"I felt so sorry for him I awoke it." And they all laughed at her.

"Vargas?" Slocum asked. "Is he the worst bandit around here?"

"No, there are others," Mucho said, shaking her head. "I don't think he would have shot Ray."

"Why not?"

She shrugged. "He is a bandit, but he don't beat up *putas*. Like tonight, you see, he went away when she said we were not working. He's not mean and cruel."

"Don't listen to her, Slocum. Mucho likes him," Pearl teased. "But Vargas is no threat."

"Who is?"

"The worst one?" Tuey asked, then checked with the others who nodded at her to go ahead.

"Cicatrize," she said in a hushed voice.

"Who's he?"

Pearl rose up, unbuttoned her dress and showed the scars on her large breasts. "The one who did that to me."

Tuey looked with displeasure at him and then shook her head. She rose, hoisted the dress high enough to show him the lash marks on her legs and slender butt.

"Why did he do that?" Slocum asked.

Tuey shook her head, hatred in her dark eyes. "He needs no reason."

The others agreed as she took her place on the floor.

"And you have no protection?" he asked.

"He would only beat us worse."

"Does he come here often?"

"He is like the wind. You never know."

"Was he here in Estria the night before? The night before Ray was killed?" Slocum looked around the room for their answer.

"We think so," Pearl said at last, indicating for Tuey to speak.

"I was busy in bed that night with a customer," Tuey began. "But once I saw his shadow in the window and it scared me so bad I about screamed."

"He didn't come back later?"

"When my customer left, I barred the doors and the windows and sat up all night with a *pistola* in my lap."

"What does he look like?"

"He has a bad scar across his face from his eye to his mouth," Pearl said, showing him on the right side of her face.

"His head is always shaved and he seldom wears a sombrero except on his back."

"*El gato*—" Tuey said. "He is like a big cat. Silent and cunning and very mean."

"The Comanches cut him when he was boy and he has no balls," Mucho said. "But he is like a proud cut horse— he gets hard, but never gets any relief, so then he gets mad and blames one of us."

Tuey nodded and the others joined her in solemn agreement.

"Where does he live?"

"They say in a cave in the mountains. No one knows," Pearl said, grasping her own arms to control a shudder of revulsion. "Just so he never ever comes back here again."

The girls crossed themselves.

Slocum nodded, deep in thought. *Putas* sometimes knew more than anyone about men, especially men they slept with. Somehow they exposed their vulnerabilities and raw nature toward one of them quicker than they did to anyone else. Even cowards whipped up on whores—why not, what could they do about it?

He needed the map that Linda must have hidden somewhere in the hovel. If there was more gold there, then she could decide on the division of it, but he owed a dead man that much effort.

Pearl was spreading out a blanket on the floor. "We are all staying here for the night. Who are you sleeping with?"

Slocum looked around the room at their faces. "I surely could not choose. You three must do that."

"Good, then all three of us," Mucho said and began to undress.

"Better get your clothes off, cowboy," Tuey said and rose to unbutton her dress. "You've got a big job ahead of you."

"Yes, ma'am," he said.

Buxom Pearl came first. His shadow loomed large on the wall as the flames in the fire heated the other side of his bare skin and he waded on his knees up between her inviting dark legs. She proved to be a butt-scooter who wanted all of him inside, and her inner walls soon were tighter than most in her profession. Signs of her effort soon approached a summit as he pumped away. Then she gave a short cry and collapsed.

Dreamy eyed, she shook her head. "You did good."

Then came Mucho, who in the shadowy light gave him a challenging look as he climbed over her legs and once between them pushed his throbbing tool into her wet gates.

"You are *grande*," she said, sounding impressed and drew a deep breath at his full stroke inside her.

In minutes, she was crying out, "Yes, yes" with each drive. Her breath quickened and she grasped his hard butt in her hands, pulling him as deep as she could. At long last she arched her back and raised him inches off the pallet with her thrust toward him, and then she fainted in a heap.

Slocum drew a deep breath and in the dimly lit room, he looked over at the last one. Maybe he could rest a minute, but she spread her slender legs wide apart and beckoned to him with her finger.

Tuey laughed aloud when they finally managed to copulate. She reminded him of a snake, slippery and sleek. He braced himself over her and soon was screwing her as hard as he could. Her fingernails were raking his back. Her sinewy legs were wrapped tight around him and she pulled him down to crush her small breasts which felt like nails going into his chest. Then he, at last, felt the pain of his ejection begin to rise in his testicles and he crushed his pelvic bone hard to hers. Come flew out the shaft like the barrel of a cannon exploding at the head and caused Tuey to yip like a coyote. They collapsed on the blanket.

And there Slocum slept in a pile of bare breasts, arms, legs, butts and an occasional check by one of them to see if his manhood had been restored.

3

In the cool morning breeze, Slocum drained his bladder outside the *jacal*. It hurt even to pee, he decided. Whew, three woman had about worn him down. The sun wasn't up yet and they were all asleep inside on the pallet. He could see the church belfry and felt satisfied that Ray had gone on to his rewards with his remains properly interred.

"You had plenty of company last night," Linda said, coming from the doorway behind him wrapped in the blanket.

"Plenty." He laughed softly. "Are you better today?"

"Yes." She went around the juniper to relieve herself and soon returned, redoing the blanket tighter to her body.

"Ray leave you a map to his mine?" he asked, looking around to be certain they were alone.

"Yes, he did."

"He tell you much?"

"Said there was lots of gold left up there and if he didn't come back for me to go get it."

"Do you need some help finding it?"

She nodded and put her fingers to his lips to silence him. "We can talk more later."

"Fine, I'm not going anywhere."

16

"Good," she said, and smiled knowingly at him. "I can't believe you did that to all three of them." Then she shook her head in disbelief.

"What?" he asked, rubbing the beard stubble on his upper lip.

"Taking on all three of those girls."

"It had been awhile."

"Must have been. Did Ray say anything else to you?"

"Just you had the—" he lowered his voice. "Map."

"He was coming back to marry me—he said."

"I'm sorry. He acted concerned that I should come here and see about you."

She turned her back to him and nodded her head that she had heard him. "I guess it was too big of a dream."

"If there's much gold it might set you up."

"Maybe—"

"The girls think some bandito named Cicatrize killed him."

"He is a bad hombre. I better go inside and get breakfast ready."

Slocum looked around and then agreed. He followed her through the back door. She went into the lean-to and shortly came back dressed. No doubt Ray had made a good choice—she was very attractive, with a shapely figure in a five-foot-tall body.

After breakfast, the *putas* split up to go about their own business after hugging Linda and giving her their sympathies. Slocum left her to check on the dun horse and to see what was happening at the cantina. He found the gelding had plenty of hay at the place Ruel had taken him to be boarded. After currying and brushing him down, Slocum went up to the Palacio Reale and ordered a beer.

"No dead men today?" Cordova, the bartender, asked him, delivering his foaming mug.

"No."

"That is good. I had nightmares all night about him."
Cordova showed signs of visibly being upset by the mere
thought of the dead man.

"Was Ray a good customer?"

"Sometimes he came in here. Mostly he went to see the
putas."

"Anyone in particular?"

"He liked Linda the most, but if she was busy he would
find another."

"Oh, I see. He must have been a horny guy?"

"When most guys arrive here they are horny. Might be
the altitude. Or whatever. Last night that whole bunch with
Vargas cussed all evening long in here because those girls
were all up there with Linda, instead of in their own shacks
working."

"They ride on?"

"Yeah, outlaws can't sleep nowhere for very long or the
ruralists will catch them."

"They ever come here? The ruralists?"

"Not often, but they can and they will."

"You ever hear of an outlaw called Cicatrize?"

The bartender looked all around to be certain they were
alone. Then with a nod in a whisper he leaned over the bar.
"He is a madman. He rapes women, cuts throats and he
even—cornholes the men he don't like."

"Who did he do that to?"

The bartender looked uncertain that he should tell
Slocum, then at last he said, "You can tell no one—he did
it to Vargas."

"He did him?"

"Yes, Vargas is more afraid of Cicatrize than he is the
ruralist. But don't tell him I told you about that."

Slocum agreed and sipped on his beer. So not only did
this bad one put fear in the hearts of the teenage *putas* of
Estria, but grown men as well. He must be a tough hombre.

If he was going to help Linda find the mine, then he'd

need to be on the lookout for this bad one. No doubt he had never been able to track Ray to his mining operation. So if she went to find it the outlaw would be on her tracks. Or perhaps this outlaw already knew and had gone back there to work it—another thing to watch out for. Plenty to think about. All he knew and had heard about Cicatrize was to be careful of him and that he was like smoke, expect him anywhere.

After his beer, he hiked up the hillside to Linda's *jacal*. She was busy packing things and startled, looked up at him.

"Sorry," he said and squatted down beside where she was putting some things in a small pannier.

"Oh, I guess I am nervous. They say the bad one has been around here."

"I've been learning about him."

"He is the cruelest one on earth."

"The girls said so last night, while you slept."

"If they wanted to go with us, would you take all of us?" she asked.

"You intend to share the gold?"

"Yes, if there is as much gold in the mine as he said, there is plenty for all of us."

"Can they shoot?"

"I don't know."

"If only you and I go that would be fine, but a train of people up in the mountains would be much harder to protect unless they were armed and could fight."

"We will meet this afternoon and you can ask them yourself."

"Fine. Should I go see about a few pack mules?"

"Good idea."

"What will you ride?"

"Oh, I can ride a horse."

"Do you have one?"

"No."

"Fine, I need a few pack mules and a horse for you."

"Do you need money?"

He rose and shook his head. "Not yet."

She stood, fluffing her full skirt so it fell over her petticoats and looked hard at him. "Then I shall kiss you until you return."

"If they can't shoot, then we may need to teach them how before we leave."

"You can ask them how good they are at the meeting." She stood on her toes and turned her pursed lips up for him.

He kissed her and felt her lithe body against his own. When he finished, a pleased smile crept on her face as she lowered herself to standing flat in her moccasins. "You won't regret what you are doing for me. I plan to pay you a full share of the gold."

"Thanks," he said.

4

A cloud of black powder smoke floated away from the four women as they hastily reloaded their cap-and-ball pistols. Slocum sent the boy Ruel to run up the hillside to set up new brown bottles to replace the shattered ones.

Linda had hit three out of five. Mucho hit two bottles, and came close enough to have winged her victim on others. Tuey shot up four of her five and obviously was no stranger to firearms. Pearl closed her eyes every time that she pulled the trigger and her setups were all standing.

"Ruel, you hold Pearl's hand and show her how again," he told the youth.

"Sure, boss." And the youth was over beside her holding her gun hand up and talking about aiming.

"My ears are ringing," Mucho complained. She looked around for some support from the others. "How much more do we have to shoot?"

Pearl's first shot blew a bottle to brown smithereens and Ruel nodded hard at her. Obviously he was pleased to be so close to a sweet-smelling older woman and so intimate with her. No telling what he would tell the other boys about his experiences.

"Get back to shooting," Linda told Mucho and slapped her on the fanny going by.

"How good do we have to be?" Linda asked him as she prepared to shoot again.

"Every outlaw in these mountains is going to know what we're going after and want a piece of the gold—you want to live you better be able to shoot a cat's eye out."

The next three shots: Linda busted bottles, missed one and made the last one right. She turned to him with a provocative look in her eye. "Better?"

"Getting that way." He smiled and the others fired away.

In three days, they were shooting with enough proficiency so that he felt certain they would be a force to be reckoned with. He let them have the rest of the day off after they scrubbed their weapons in boiling soapy water to clean all the residue out of the cylinders and barrel, dried, oiled and loaded them.

He told Linda he would see her later; he planned to ride down the valley and look up a man with four pack mules for sale. She agreed and asked if he needed any money yet. He shrugged off her concern, and was joined by his helper Ruel, on horseback, who had brought him the dun. They set off down the trail to get back to the road. He had tried to use an isolated canyon for their gun range, hoping to attract less attention. Still he knew his "petticoat army" was no secret in Estria. Nothing he could do about that, but possibly get himself shot by some horny guy for taking the town's entire whore population with him when he left. The notion amused him.

"You ever have so many women pistoleers before?" Ruel asked, with a mischievous grin.

Slocum shook his head. "No, I haven't. What do you think?"

"Oh, señor, I like them."

"That's good. We better trot these horses or we won't get to this man's casa before dark."

They found the farmer busy working in his bean field and he came up the row with his hoe, leaving his wife and several children to chop the weeds.

"Diego is my name, señor."

"Slocum is mine; you know Ruel?"

The short man nodded and wiped his sweaty face on his sleeve. "I have four good mules—they will pack or work. Anything you need them for."

"Four good mules is a lot to have in one place," Slocum said, amused at his own words. Also hard to believe.

"These have all been packed on and I worked them in my crops."

"Good." Slocum leaned over the corral and looked at the sleepy hybrids. Not hinnies, but all mules—good, he liked them. They bore white pack-saddle scars on their withers and none were showing any sign of age.

"How much?" he asked.

"Ten pesos apiece."

"Five."

"Oh, señor, that is too cheap."

Slocum dropped his gaze to the ground and shook his head. "Ten apiece is too much."

"I would sell them for thirty pesos."

"Twenty-six?"

"No, I would keep them." The man shook his head.

"Twenty-eight."

"You are a hard man to do business with, señor. I would take twenty-eight for them."

So Slocum and his entourage left the next morning, the four women wearing pants under their skirts, wide sombreros on their heads and riding horses. Slocum took the lead and they tended to the braying pack string. He hoped he had everything that they needed in the panniers under the canvas-covered diamonds hitched over their backs. Going over the hill from the village, he twisted in the saddle and studied his crew.

Mucho led the mules and Tuey rode in with a quirt, making them step out. The slender part-Indian girl looked as if she had been born in the saddle as she crowded her pony in close and lashed at the errant ones. Her cries at the laggard pack animals sounded like coyote yips.

Still acting withdrawn, wrapped in a colorful blanket, Linda rode a dainty stepping, small sorrel horse he had bought for her. An obviously well-bred animal, its gait was a rolling one.

Mucho sat aboard a flea-bitten gray, long headed and dull acting. She constantly used her rowels on him and cursed Vargas for bringing her such a sorry one to ride. Even in the dress of a man, her firm breasts jiggled under the shirt, the deep brown cleavage exposed from the open buttons. Closed, however, they would have stressed the material too much.

Buxom Pearl rode a slab-sided pony behind Linda. Another dull-eyed brown mustang, but she beat a tattoo on his sloping hips with a stick to make him keep up. Her long black hair swept back and tied with rawhide cord, she looked at ease in the saddle and capable of moving out if necessary.

All of them were armed. He felt they were good enough shots to handle any problem and could handily use their sidearms. Besides his rifle, Tuey carried a sword in her scabbard. She could shoot the lever action, too.

By his judgement of Ray's map, they would have three to four days riding around the face of the mother mountains to reach the area. Then Slocum could hope that the vague details of pencil on paper would lead them to the mine. What looked informative to the mapmaker sometimes left the ones looking for something to search over hundreds of acres. Something niggled him: If there was so much gold there for the taking, why didn't claim jumpers pile in when he left and steal a lot? Maybe they were already there doing that.

And what about Cicatrize? How much did the robbery-murder yield to him? Good question? No answer. Linda had mentioned that Ray had a large amount of gold on him. Then Slocum smiled at a scolding black-and-white camprobber on the limb of a pine. When they rounded the next point he could see for miles across the desert far below. Fluffy clouds were beginning to gather. The formation would build until midafternoon, then somewhere in the range they would rumble and roar like the devil dancing and drench the dry earth. Monsoons that would cool the sharp mountain's breath and perhaps drive the altitude headache from his forehead. This, too would pass in a few more days in the sky, him getting acclimated to the thinner air.

Tuey's yipping, the clop of horse hooves, the squeak of leather, it all blended with the girls' voices as they teased one another. He tried to be alert. Not only were there out-laws in these ranges, but hostile Apaches, the remnant of Geronimo's Chirichua tribe that refused repatriation and Florida prison were roaming the land. At times, it was listed as hundreds of them left behind, but the U.S. Army officially scoffed and spoke of only a handful of them.

One evening, stopping over at the San Bernadino ranch house on the border, Slocum had shared some good whiskey and a fine cigar with a rancher, John Slaughter. The two men sat on the main house's veranda, where they overlooked the spring-fed lake and Slaughter's farmland that stretched far down into Mexico.

When the time seemed right, Slocum asked the man, "How many bronco Apaches are left down here?"

Slaughter nodded. He wore a trimmed mustache and sharp beard that moved when he talked. "Hundred twenty to fifty."

"But the Army said—"

"Christ, they never knew. They only counted the ones that went to San Carlos at one time or the other and regis-tered. This bunch was down there. They were under Who.

Close kin to the Cherrycows, but another branch. So when the Army got that sneaky coyote Geronimo, they wrote the rest off as Mexican Injuns." Slaughter shook his gray head as if upset with the whole thing. "That bastard Miles had to cover his ass. He wouldn't have made a wart on Crook's backside. When the damn Tucson Ring's man got Geronimo drunk and he run off, Sheridan was pissed.

"So he fired Crook and brought that pompous ass Miles down here with ten thousand more soldiers and fired all the Apache scouts. Men like Tom Horn knew more about them red devils than Miles or his staff even could count." Slaughter poured more whiskey in Slocum's glass.

"Drink up. You're lucky you don't have livestock down here. Game's so thin, they eat my cattle like they were rabbits. Oh, I raid their camps and run them back to the Madras, but they're back in no time."

Slocum drew on the cigar and then let the smoke out. "In the end the Apache scouts and two lieutenants got them to come out. Miles got all the credit and never mentioned a damn thing the others did, including the Apache scouts he put on the train with the hostiles—bastard!"

"Why ain't they any worse?"

"Them Apaches that are left? Hell, they don't have a good leader. Who was a tough one. Real strategist. They say he died of a heart attack or was plain drunk, then fell in a river and drowned. Geronimo was a damn *bruja*. Sumbitch could foresee things better than most witches. When they lost them two, no one else could ever lead or do those things."

Slaughter's young wife came out and smiled at Slocum in the twilight. She put a shawl on John's shoulders, remarking it was getting cool outside and they should not stay out there much longer.

"Yes, dear," he said after her, and in the growing darkness shook his head. "Damn, think I was a child. Have you seen Horn lately?"

Slocum shook his head. "No, it's been a few years."

"Working for Pinkerton now, I guess. You see him, tell him to stop by. He can talk their lingo. He might strike a deal with them broncos for me. I'd give them a few head of cattle to eat, but I hate like hell to see one they've only took a loin or leg off of and left the rest to the damn buzzards."

Slocum agreed. "You ready to go inside?"

"Hell, no. I don't get many visitors from the old days drifting by here anymore and get a chance to talk to them." He raised his glass. "To the old days."

"Yes," Slocum said and they clinked their drinks.

5

He cut back their travel around noon the first day. Clouds were boiling up like it aimed to slam into them. He picked a grassy flat and went to setting off packs. Everyone worked. Mucho and Tuey stripped off the diamond hitches and canvas. Linda and Pearl began bringing in armloads of firewood.

Slocum could smell the rain coming out of the south. The grumble in the belly of the storm grew louder every minute. A tent was soon out and Tuey drove stakes. The others screwed tent poles together. A gust of wind threatened to take the whole thing away from them, but they fought and won the tug-of-war. The canvas structure soon emerged and Slocum used all of his weight to pull the ropes on the windward side while they hooked them over the stakes and drew them snug. The girls had the opposite side worked tight and they headed inside.

Slocum looked at the panniers, all canvas-covered and looking secure. The bug-eyed mules that spooked at every flash wouldn't leave the hobbled sorrel mare. Cold drops began to penetrate his shirt when he ducked inside. The women in the dim light were rolling out bedrolls and talking like magpies.

"Will it be a bad storm?" Pearl asked, looking concerned at the yellow cloth walls being peppered with hard rain.

"Be a wet one for sure." He laughed and they all shook their heads at his indifference to Mother Nature's fury.

"You know about these storms—" Mucho's words were cut off by the lightning strike close by that shook the ground underneath them.

"That was too close." He frowned, straightening up again. "You all did great in the first test," he said and dropped to his haunches. "We did everything close to right."

"What did we forget?" Pearl asked.

"Our rifles are out there with our saddles under the canvas, which is fine, but we needed to have them in here." He pointed at the ground between his boots.

"I never thought anyone smart would be out in this weather," Linda said.

"That's what they'd want you to think."

His words drew knowing nods from them.

"We'll do better next time," Mucho promised and they all agreed.

"Hey, let's face it. If Ray's mine is as rich as he said it was, there will be lots of folks looking to take it from you. Savvy?"

"What do you think about his mine?" Tuey asked, sitting cross-legged on the ground and picking at the dry grass stems around her.

"It must have been—" A blinding flash and nearby crash cut him off for a second. "A real mine. He got his gold somewhere."

"That brings up something else," Linda said. "I don't trust Vargas. He never asked Pearl or Mucho about why they needed their horses. Just smiled at them like a shit-eating cur and delivered them like he expected more than a piece of ass or two for his deed."

"What do you think?" Slocum asked Mucho.

"Well, if that little cockerel come scratching around for anything more than a few humps, I'll wring his scrawny neck. Besides, those dumb horses he gave us weren't worth one good screwing."

Pearl agreed. "We all know him. He brags how big his dick is and it isn't so."

They laughed. Then Tuey held her brown fingers a few inches apart to demonstrate the size of it and they laughed again with a loud, "Yes."

The rain grew steadier on the canvas and the wind had subsided some from the hard breaths that had threatened the sidewalls. Thunder sounded more distant.

Slocum stuck his head out and could see the clearing sky moving toward them.

"Be over in a few minutes."

"Good, my ass is galled from that saddle," Pearl said. "I am sitting my butt in that small creek and soaking it."

"May have to wait a little," Slocum said. "It's belching full right now."

He headed out the front flap as the storm waned. The cool, clean air filled his lungs and he stretched his arms over his head. It felt good to be up in the mountains. A damn sight cooler than down in the border country, and a lot less stressful than wondering who'd walk in next with a Wanted poster for him. A few final drops struck him. He pointed out to the emerging girls a smoldering pine top, high on the slope above them, that had made the hard crash and where lightning had split off half of its height, the top twenty feet lay on the ground at the base.

Pearl, armed with a towel, went past, headed for the small creek. But not before she made a wicked wink at him. Tuey set in to build a fire. Mucho was getting ready to make tortillas, hand-mixing flour, lard and water into a thick dough. Linda finally emerged and nodded to him, then she joined in the fire-building.

Slocum found the rifles and set one by the log where they were building the fire, the other one inside the tent. Shifting the holster on his right hip, he headed for a high spot with his telescope to look over the land.

He could see for miles, looking for a trace of smoke, a telltale reflection off a silver concha. But he saw nothing out of the ordinary. Tuey joined him. She dropped down on her stomach beside him and began to chew on a stem of grass.

"Anything in that glass?"

"No. Are there any Apaches up here?"

She nodded. "Small bands. So their camps are harder to find. The Mexican army searches for them all the time. They have what you call bounty men, too. They look for them. They shoot woman, children. Who cares, huh?"

"I'm surprised the army comes up here."

She smiled faintly. "They have a few brave ones." She chuckled. "Not many. The broncos' biggest enemies are those bounty men."

"Did you live up here?"

"As a small girl, I came with my mother down here from San Carlos."

"Why did you come back down here, then?"

"My father was a Chiricahua. My mother was a captive from Mexico and she married him. When he was killed in the fighting, the other squaws at San Carlos said she should go live with her own people because she was so pretty they hated her."

"What did she do?"

"She came back to Mexico, but her people were all dead and the women down there said she was an Apache *puta*. So she became one. I was an outcast, too."

"Those men in the village didn't seem to mind you being part Apache."

"Ha," she said, then closed her lips on the straw as if in deep thought. At last she turned to him with a mischievous smile. "They could go fuck a donkey, if they didn't like me, huh? I guess I am better than that."

"Much better," Slocum said, collapsing his telescope. "Have we crossed any sign of the broncos since we started this direction?"

"I saw some about midday when we crossed the valley back there."

"What was it?"

"Three unshod horses. It was over a day old."

"Good, but they might stumble on us."

"I will watch more careful," she said, pushing herself up to her knees.

"I'd appreciate that. What will you do with your share?"

"Buy me lots of Navaho silver and turquoise jewelry, red silk dresses, big hats with feathers, dog leather shoes and get me a fancy team of horses and a surrey with a full-blood Apache driver in a top hat and tuxedo. Then I will go back to San Carlos and spit on all those sons of bitches that ran my mother away."

Amused, Slocum chuckled aloud, imagining the sight of her and her outfit stopping at each wickiup and shouting for them to come out, so she could pucker up and spit at them.

"They might shoot you." He chuckled.

"Oh, I'd have this pistol you got for me, and I can use it."

"Yes, you can," he agreed, and threw his arm over her shoulder, and despite their difference in height, she went along, bumping her hip into him as they walked back to camp.

The horses and mules hobbled and grazed, with nothing out of place or they'd be looking—especially the mules. A mule deer on the move could catch a mule's keen eyesight. The mare wouldn't miss much either. Slocum used them as his own eyes.

Linda came from the small cooking fire with a cup of coffee for him. "Anything?"

"No. Tuey saw some signs coming up here. But it might mean nothing."

She squinted her eyes against the strong sun and nodded. "I knew these mountains were big, but I had no idea they were this vast."

"That's why Geronimo could hide from all the armies after him and only Apache scouts ever found him."

"I see why now. We have a two-day ride left?"

"Yes, we should get there by then. I'm being cautious. There may be men on our backtrail. I don't want them to jump us at the mine."

She nodded in approval. "Why would you do all this for four *putas*?"

"Let's say I was out of work."

She laughed and shook her head. "You sure aren't out of pussy."

"I guess you could call that the benefit to this job."

Her brown eyes clouded with not understanding; she wrinkled her nose at his words.

"My bonus for being here."

They both laughed.

After sundown, they all went to find their blankets. For the last time, he made a wide circle of the camp and satisfied, squatted on his boot heels to smoke a cigarette by himself. The roll-your-own between his fingers, he inhaled deep to let the nicotine relax him. At last finished, he snuffed it out and shredded the rest. Stiff in the back, he rose and went to find his blankets.

Overhead, a blanket of stars began to pop out. Night insects played a concert when he shed his boots while seated on the bedroll. The relief of his stocking feet escaping the footwear felt good, wiggling his toes. He rose up, flipped back the covers and settled down. This high up, he'd need all of his covers before dawn. In the morning, he must . . .

"Wake up!' a voice loaded with urgency hissed in his ear. He discovered someone was bellied down beside him.

His fingers closed on the Colt's grip under the covers. A woman's musk reached his nose, when she spoke again.

"We got company out there. Move slow."

6

Who in the hell was out there? On his side, Slocum eased on his boots. In the pearly starlight, he could see Tuey's dark eyes searching the night.

"Apaches or outlaws?"

"Outlaws, maybe."

"How many?"

"I heard a strange horse snort a short while ago and it woke me up."

He nodded in approval, still unable to make out any forms, save the horses' silhouettes in the meadow that was better lit than under the pines where the camp was.

"Get up slow and follow me," she said, getting on her knees.

In a swish, she disappeared in the thicker timber. Gun in hand, he followed her. Grateful to be standing, they stopped in the midst of the thicker trunks.

She gave a head toss for him to look toward the meadow. Two men were coming downhill, headed for the horses. They wore Chihuahua peaked sombreros and made their moves cautious enough, despite being in the open. They kept twisting around, searching for any guards.

"I need the rifle," Slocum whispered.

When Slocum looked for her again, she was gone. Where did she go? He knew the range was too far for his handgun. But it might scare them off. Only thing wrong with scaring them off was they'd be back another day to try to steal his animals again.

In a few minutes, she was back and handed him the rifle.

"Thanks. Only an Apache could have done that," he said softly and put the rifle's barrel against the tree to steady his shot. Through the buckhorn sights, he took the figure on the right. His thumb cocked the hammer back and he held his breath with the rifle steady on the target. A finger squeezed off the shot. An orange fire belched out the muzzle and the raider's hands flew in the air. Slocum could see the cloud of acrid smoke from the powder. The blast reverberated across the mountains and back.

Levering in a cartridge, he took a new spot to shoot from and drew a bead on the other fleeing outlaw's figure about to reach the timber's shadows. The .44/40 spoke again and the struck man screamed in the night.

Then a drum of hooves was coming off the mountain. Slocum stepped out in the edge of the trees' shade, so he could better make out the attacker. A lone hatless rider firing two pistols at him screamed like a banshee as he charged.

Slocum used the safety of the first tree. Exploded bark rained down on his head in the barrage of hot lead. Bullets thudded into the ponderosa and the rider swept by. Slocum knelt and fired after him until the hammer fell on the empty chamber. Then he listened to the man's maniacal laughter and his horse's hooves pounding off into the night.

"Cicatrize," she said.

He nodded that he heard her. "We better go see about the others."

"They will be nervous. All this shooting."

"What's happened?" was the first question as the other

women in their nightclothes and armed with their pistols met them returning.

"I guess Cicatrize tried to steal the horses."

"Oh, no," Mucho said and shook her head. "Did you kill him?"

"No, but he shot two of his men," Tuey said.

"I better go check on them," Slocum said. A wounded rattler was worse sometimes than a freed one.

"We all want to go," Linda said.

"No, the three of you stay here and guard camp. Besides, it may not be nice up there."

"You think he'll be back tonight?" Pearl asked.

Slocum shook his head. "But we better be on our guard. He has in his mind because you are women, he can take what he wants."

"He's got another thing coming," Mucho said.

"I agree, but I don't want to lose our supplies or anything. He never realized the horses were hobbled and planned to drive them out with his charge. Come on, Tuey, let's go see about those two."

"Be careful," Linda said, sounding put out by the whole affair.

"We will." The two set out in a lope for the meadow.

Their appearance forced the animals to look up. Slocum discovered the first outlaw lying facedown. With care, he rolled him over. The man's blank eyes stared at the sky. Dead.

She went on to the next one before Slocum could say a word to caution her.

"Come." She motioned to him. "This one is still alive."

Slocum nodded. He had never seen the first dead man before, but perhaps the others would know him.

Standing on the slope above the stricken outlaw, he agreed with her there still was life in this bandit lying on his back. A dark spot was on his shirt where the blood stained the cloth.

"Who are you?"

"Renalto—Castro." The man's words were said with pain.

"What did you intend to do with our horses?"

"We thought they were runaways."

"Liar, you came to steal them," she hissed at him. A small knife was in her fist. She waved it in his face. "You want me to cut out your *huevos*?"

"No."

"Where is Cicatrize's camp?" Slocum asked, holding her back with his forearm. He needed some answers from this man.

"On the Rio Blanco." He motioned over the mountain with a head toss.

"How many men are there?"

"A dozen."

"No more?"

"No more."

"Why do you work for such a bastard?" she demanded.

"It is a job." The man shrugged.

"How many innocent women have you raped?"

"None. I never—"

"Let me have him. I want to make his last hours on this earth as hard on him as he has made it on the poor girls he preyed upon."

"What if I say no?"

"Who is he to you?" She glared at him in defiance.

Slocum had no answer for her. He swept up the man's handgun off the ground, took two knives from the scabbards on him.

"Señor, Mother of God. Please don't leave me with her," Castro begged.

"I think when you chose to ride with Cicatrize, you never expected to fall in such hands. But I am outvoted in this camp by angry women. Where are your horses?" He looked around in the night for them.

"You can't!" His desperate plea shattered the air.

"I'll find them," he said, more to himself than to her or to the fear-stricken outlaw and started uphill to look for them. He shut his ears to Castro's cries and began to climb the slope for the timber. They'd be tethered up there somewhere.

In a short while he found the two hipshot horses. Castro's cries reverberated off the towering ranges.

7

Dawn glowed on the tops of the highest peaks. A soft light filtered through the evergreen bough canopy overhead. Noisy camprobbers and ravens hollered at them as they glided around to better see his invasionary force. Slocum led the way on the dun, and behind him came the pack mules, spare horses and the four women dispersed in the line, whacking lazy mules and being certain they stayed in close.

Knowledge that the outlaw Cicatrize knew they were in the mountain had made the women act more somber. They put their hands on their gun butts more often, adjusting how their holsters rode on their hips, checking the caps on the cylinders. Wary would have been a good word, he decided, for their readiness—which suited him. They faced a powerful enemy—who had ghostlike qualities about him that made his threat even more sinister to the women.

How many of these four had he raped and beat up? Some had already shown him their scars from his unbridled viciousness. While his own wild shooting in the dark of the night before had not brought the outlaw down, he carried no conceptions that this one was supernatural. But he felt the madman was extremely cunning and would be hard to match wits with before their odyssey was over. This situation could only end one way. One of them would be dead.

At noontime, they paused at a stream, and the women caught a mess of small silver trout for lunch. The fast action of fishing, and Pearl falling in the water to her neck, revived their humor. Slocum cleaned and reloaded her revolver while they bathed and took turns cooking fish.

Seated on the ground with his back to a small cottonwood, he looked up from his work occasionally to observe the turn of a bare hip or the beads of water on a pear shaped breast. Dark rings of a silver-dollar-sized brown nipple peering from the white soapy lather. The shiny wet black triangle at the crossroads of where her legs split. All the sights of brown to olive-oil-colored skin distracted him at times from his gunsmith work.

"You could use a bath, too," Mucho said with a frown for him.

"Are you asserting I smell like a horse?" he asked as if amazed by her question.

In Spanish she asked for a translation.

"He wants to know does his horse dick need to be washed," Linda said in Spanish and laughed.

"*Sí*," Mucho said and began to wade toward him with a deliberate look in her dark eyes.

No mistaking her purpose, he lay down the gun he was working on and, holding them off with one hand, began to toe off his boots. Stripped down to his underwear, three of them shoved him off the bank into the cold stream. He came up dripping water and saw Tuey come running with her rifle in hand.

"Someone is coming!"

Everyone went for their sidearms and knelt down, trying to see who she spoke about. Slocum dried his hands on his shirt and took up the rifle leaning against a log.

"Who is it?"" Linda hissed.

Slocum shook his head, unable to see anyone. He motioned to Tuey, who shrugged. "I heard someone coughing. There!"

Slocum frowned at the hatless man who staggered up the trail waving his hands and shouting, "*Amigos! Amigos! Don't shoot. It is me, Vargas!*"

Then he fell to his knees and bent over coughing.

"What is he doing here?" Linda demanded.

"We never told him anything," Mucho said, pulling on her skirt.

"Better question is what do we do with him?" Slocum said.

Sprawled on his side, Vargas held up his hand to defend himself. "I mean no harm. But I must escape that damn Cicatrize."

"You saw him?" Slocum asked.

"*Sí*, he killed Blondie and Waco. I barely got away with my life."

"Oh, not Blondie?" Pearl said and shook her head in sadness.

"He was a good hombre. He never meant that bastard no harm." Vargas shook his head as if upset, too.

"You girls decide what to do with him," Slocum said and scowled at the outlaw. "Shoot him, send him back or take him along. Whatever."

"I give you the horses you asked for—"

Slocum went back to finish his bath. They got many more camp followers and the word got out, the whole Mexican army would be up there to investigate.

In a few minutes, Linda came and sat down by the stream.

Slocum, naked and knee deep in the water, looked at her for the answer to their latest visitor.

"We decided another gun wouldn't hurt. I'll personally shoot him if he messes up."

"I hope he's some good somewhere that I haven't seen." He went back to lathering his chest with the soap.

They camped later in the afternoon after the long fish cooking break at noon. The girls gathered firewood and Slocum made a wide circle with Tuey, looking for any sign in the area.

"You didn't approve of Vargas staying," she said as they led their horses, searching the ground for any signs.

"He's a two-bit outlaw. All he wants is for us to save his ass from Cicatrize cornholing him again and to get off with the gold."

"I promise you he tries anything, I'll make a steer out of him."

"Just so he don't kill one of us in the process. That's my worry. I trust him far as I can throw him."

"Another day and we will be at the mine. What if Cicatrize is there waiting for us?"

"Reckon he's got a special suit picked out?"

"Why?" Her dark eyes flashed the question at him.

"Most folks like to be buried in nice clothing."

Laughing aloud, she shook her head in disbelief. "He doesn't scare you?"

"No. Does he scare you?"

She closed her eyes. "The night he trapped me in that room and I had no knife, no gun, yes."

"He comes around, we may show him fear."

"Good idea, we better get back. They may have food ready by now."

"No Apache signs today?"

She shook her head and mounted her pony in a quick leap. "Nothing. Funny, we did not see his tracks coming up this way."

"Maybe he came over the hill."

She shrugged. "Don't sleep too tight tonight, you may have company, big man."

"Fine." He mounted and headed after her for camp.

Slocum sat cross-legged on the ground, eating his beans by the campfire light when Linda came over and took a place beside him.

"Sorry I went against your wishes today."

He glanced over at her. "Your show."

"Ah, but we might not be alive if we hadn't had you when Cicatrize came."

"He taught you and the others another lesson. Be on your guard at all times."

She nodded. "Yes, we all carry our pistols now and keep the rifles close by."

Slocum glanced across the fire to where Vargas was talking loudly with Pearl and Mucho. The two women acted entertained. Slocum lowered his voice. "Remember, trust him as far as you can throw him."

Linda gave a sober look in Vargas's direction and nodded. "You think he will try something."

"When we find the mine, you watch him close. Greed is a bad disease. It corrupts the mind."

"*Sí.*" She nodded her head woodenly. "I'll warn Mucho. She will understand. Pearl would argue with me."

"Do what you must."

"Slocum?"

"Yes."

"I appreciate all you have done for us. I will pay you back—somehow."

He shook his head to dismiss her concern and spooned more beans in his mouth to slowly masticate. Vargas's laughter and bravado made his stomach turn. Slocum knew his kind; the man would be a slinking coyote coward when the chips were down and the tables turned against him.

His plate empty, Slocum put his utensils in the boiling water and nodded to Mucho, who was in charge of them.

"Will the bad one come back tonight?" she asked under

her breath. The firelight danced in her worried-looking brown eyes.

"If it suits him."

"Should we post guards?"

"If I think he's about, I'll wake someone to do that later."

"I would be glad to do my part."

"*Gracias.* Get some sleep. There is no telling about what we'll find at the mine, *mañana.*"

"You think he is there?"

"Claim jumpers come in all forms."

Slocum searched around the campfire for Vargas, but he and Pearl were out of sight. No doubt taking advantage of the situation.

"Good night," Slocum said and swept up his rifle.

The soft night wind in the pines hummed a lullaby. The strong turpentine smell in his nose, he walked on the balls of his feet in the shadowy timber, careful not to crush a stick underfoot or make any noise.

A red wolf raised his muzzle to the sky and his mournful howl carried and re-echoed off the mountainsides. Then another joined him. Soon a whole pack of the bloodthirsty killers swept over the next ridge, anxious for a meal of his mule deer. Good sign. If there had been anyone close by observing the camp, the wolves would not have been so brave.

Slocum squatted on his heels, rifle over his knees and watched the horses and mules. Most stood hipshot, sleeping on their feet, nothing bothered them. Then a soundless owl winged over the open meadow, searching for prey. Time for him to turn in and sleep a few hours.

His bedroll was far enough from the campfire to be absorbed in the darker shadows of the trees. He laid the rifle close by and unbuckled his gunbelt. When he toed off his boots, he could hear the women talking in hushed voices.

They didn't even realize that he had circled them and was at his bedroll. A small smile on his face, he reached down, covered up and sought some shut-eye.

"It is me, amigo," she whispered and laid a finger on his lips.

He awoke as Tuey slipped under the blankets to join him. His hand touched her bare skin and he realized that she was naked. Her fingers quickly undid the buttons on his fly, and she ran her hand over the mound of his manhood beneath his underwear. He pulled her facedown and kissed her.

Then a strange realization came over him: how small she really was in the buff. Woman could be short, but when they were completely undressed and in bed with a man, they suddenly became toy-sized. Her proud breasts were teacups when he molded them. The twin cheeks of her butt fit in his hands.

She undid his underwear. Soon he sat up and she stripped it away, quickly biting his shoulder as if hungry for him. They sought the warmth of the blankets again with her sprawled on top of him. Her sleek skin against him, she moved like a serpent on his muscle-corded stomach, her mouth tasting his with a new fire of abandonment.

Then she slipped lower on his body, so her hand could close around his half-hard shaft. Her hot lips kissing the skin on his chest, she began to work her fist to erect him. Soon she was between his legs, one hand kneeing his testicles, the other bringing his dick to full glory.

Satisfied, she slithered over him and lay beside so he could get up. In a flash, she was beneath him, drawing her legs up and guiding him to her berth. A cry escaped her lips when he entered her. Her legs folded to her shoulders, she arched her back to form a ball. He began pounding her. The walls of her vagina began to swell and thicken.

His breath rushed through his nose like a freight train. Heart pounding like sledgehammer, he sought more and more. Sweat ran down his sides, stung his right eye as their efforts grew wilder. Her heels locked on his shoulders, he poured it to her. Alone in a whirlwind of their own with one goal, the pace grew more frenzied. The skin on the head of his dick felt ready to burst. Then a cramp in his left nut signaled the start of the end. Great needles struck both sides of his butt and a cannon fired from the depth of his scrotum. He exploded inside her as deep as he could shove it. She groaned and collapsed in a small pile under him.

Sapped of his strength, he rose up enough to let her unfold her legs, then dropped to the pallet beside her. Her small form curled in a ball against his belly, they both slept.

8

Slocum used his brass telescope to study the mine site on the opposite side of the canyon. Belly down in the pine needles, he studied the area for any sign of activity. Nothing looked as if anyone had been there or recently worked it. Something niggled at him. The small cabin looked unused, too.

"What do you think?" Vargas asked, crawling up to get closer to him.

"Can't see anything. But I think the women should stay over here until we're sure."

"Good idea, *amigo.*" The Mexican rubbed his black bearded mouth with his cupped hand like a man full of greedy expectations and studied the deep canyon.

Slocum did not consider the man his *amigo.* Still, he liked the idea of being safe rather than sorry in their approach of the mine, even if his only helper in this case was not proven.

"We going now?"

"Better tell the women the plan. We'll be a couple of hours working our way over there."

"Ah, *sí,* tell them our plan."

They both edged back into the trees, then went down in the draw where girls and the animals rested.

"We are going to ride over there," Vargas announced. "There is none over there."

Linda nodded to the man acting like the majordomo and brought a burrito of cold beans for Slocum. She frowned as the man went on about how he had looked and done all the scouting.

"He is such a braggart." In disgust, she shook her head and handed Slocum his food. "Something to keep up your strength' "

"Vargas is a little man." He winked at her.

"But such a big mouth. Is it safe?"

"Looks that way. I couldn't see anything across the canyon or around it."

"But you sound hesitant?" Linda frowned again, looking concerned at him.

"Well, how has he kept it secret—the mine I mean? There it sits. People know he took out lots of gold. Why don't they high grade it when he is gone?"

"I'll show you when we get over there." A confident smile crossed her full lips.

He nodded and took a bite from his bean burrito.

"Where will you go after we leave here?" She stood with her arms folded over her breasts and stared toward the timber on the mountainside.

"Someplace where the tequila flows, the music is soft and the women all cook good."

"You ever been to Ancha?"

He shook his head. "Where is that?"

"Oh, it is north in the Madres. I want to buy a ranch there. It has a good stream, fine place."

"I get some time, I might drop in."

She used her right hand to lift ribbons of long dark hair and place them higher on her head. "I will have good tequila—mescal, whatever you like."

"Sounds tempting, but a man wouldn't need much if he had you."

She looked a little taken aback by his words and nodded. "I better get my horse. They look ready to leave."

"Let Vargas take the front point, we'll see how he does."

"You still don't trust him, do you?"

"Ain't been no temptation—yet. He's on his best behavior. Got all the pussy he can handle with Pearl and Mucho. Hell, the man's in paradise."

"Maybe, you're jealous?"

"Does he have you?"

"No." She frowned.

"Good." He grinned big at her. "We better get our horses and follow him."

"Why'" she asked, hurrying beside him down the slope to their animals. "Did you want me?"

He looked hard at her. "Did I say no?" With a boost, he loaded her into the saddle. "Watch yourself. That trail is narrow going around the head of this canyon."

"Tonight?" she asked over her shoulder as he mounted and swung the dun in behind her.

"Your party."

Then she laughed out loud. "We'll see about that."

The trail was one horse wide around the head of the canyon. The open strip of a half a mile came from a landslide that must have happened years earlier. All the timber had been swept down the steep hillside and the gray dirt combed with rocks grew some bunches of tickle grass and a few stunted sagebrushes.

The right place for an ambush, Slocum worried, twisting in the saddle, but seeing nothing out of place. But the trail looked inviting enough and was the one shown on the map—so Ray must have used it, too. Any other way meant a day's ride over the top and around because the mountain face above the old slide area was cut off by bluffs sheer as a cow's face.

Vargas was in the lead with the three girls; then came the mules and extra horse. Linda was fifty feet behind the last animal on her horse, and the dun with Slocum came sugar-footing along in the rear. Craning his neck around to look again for anything, he rested the Winchester on his lap. Still no way for him to be satisfied with being exposed to so much. The high sun shone down on them.

The creak of saddle leather, the soft plod of the animals hooves and the chatter of the three women filled the air.

Slocum tried to be alert—then the crack of a rifle broke the solitude of the deep canyon underneath them. A horse screamed. Vargas fell off him. His hurt animal went off the side, kicking and screaming in pain as he slid down the hillside. The train bunched.

"Ride like hell!" he shouted at the women, waving for them to go on. If one of those mules tried to turn in the path, the whole train might go off down the mountainside like Vargas's horse.

Slocum set spurs to the dun. He cat-hopped up the hillside until he turned him on an angle to come down at the front of the mules.

"Go on, girls. Head for the woods."

"Bring them on," he yelled to Linda, skidding the dun to a halt on the narrow pathway and looking a thousand feet down into the gorge. Gaining the first mule's lead, he jerked it around. The shocked, once-frozen girls had untracked for the timber a hundred yards ahead.

"Wait for me!" Wide-eyed, Vargas shouted, struggling to get his footing on the side of the slope where his horse lay dead far below.

"Come on yourself," Slocum said and took off with the mules in tow. He expected that any minute another shot would be fired and his name would be on the bullet.

Vargas jumped on behind Linda, but Slocum had no time, since he was hauling the pack train hard as he could, the rope tallied on the horn and the dun bogging down to keep them moving in a long trot.

The three girls reached the timber and he looked back to see about Linda's progress. More shots came from ahead of him. He turned back in time to see the puffs of Tuey's rifle and then heard the loud reports. He looked up in time to catch sight of someone with a sniper rifle disappearing in the timber above them.

Must have waited too long to take his first shot. After he hit Vargas's horse, they had been too far under the lip of the hill for him to get a shot at them. Good enough, Tuey's shooting had made him show himself. Though Slocum couldn't make out much about the sniper, he hoped they met again under better circumstances and he recognized him.

"You all right? You all right?" Mucho asked, running out to take the mule leads.

"Didn't kill me or Vargas," Slocum said and winked at Linda as she reined.

"Mother of God, who was that shooter?" Vargas asked, looking pale-faced at the mountain. "He about killed me and—the poor horse. . . ." The man acted thunderstruck.

"We've got another horse," Mucho said and shook her head in disapproval. "*Gracias*, Slocum. You saved us by making us move on."

"I was coming to help but I could hardly stand up," Vargas protested.

"We're all fine now and one horse is no loss compared to anyone getting hurt." He looked around for the Apache girl. "Where's Tuey?"

"Guess she went to track down the shooter," Pearl said. "I saw her take off through the timber going up the mountain."

"Linda, take everyone to the cabin. Post guards and put the animals up in the pens so they can't run them off."

"We'll set up camp."

"You need me?" Vargas asked in his bravo style.

"No, help Linda and the women," Slocum said, reining

the dun around ready to leave. "Watch close. They'll try something."

"No worry, *mi amigo*, they will be safe with me."

Mi amigo, my ass. Slocum forced back his convictions. "All of you watch out."

He set the dun uphill for the top of the mountain. The dun horse cat-hopped up the steeper sides through the scattered timber. Obvious from the stumps, many larger trees had been logged off for mine timbers and the cabin's construction.

How far had she gone? An Apache could do many things in stealth, but she might not be able to match wits with Cicatrize. The more he thought about the outlaw's reputation, the more he knew Cicatrize used so well to his own advantage the people's fear of the supernatural and witches. He reined the dun in sight of her bay, standing ground-tied. Reaching back, he jerked out his Winchester and halted the hard-breathing dun and swung off.

Nothing in sight, he hurried for the top of the ridge above him. At a soft hiss, he froze in his tracks. She held her finger to her lips and waved him over to the security of a large pine trunk.

"Three men on the other side talking." She gave a head toss to mean over the crest above them. "One is Cicatrize."

"Lets get 'em."

She gave him a firm nod and went to the right, indicating for him to go left. Then they started up the hillside. The needles were thick as a rug underfoot and a sharp-eared squirrel chattered at them. Somewhere a raven cawed.

Slocum saw their hats, then he dropped down and crawled the last twelve feet on his belly to the edge. With a ready nod to her, he raised up and began firing. The one with his back to him threw out his arms and screamed when the hot lead caught him. It was enough diversion that Cicatrize, his bald head shining in the sun, did a flip off his horse and was unseen making his way for the brush. The third man was taken down by a barrage of her bullets. The three horses panicked and jerked aside.

Slocum tried to see in the fading black powder gunsmoke where the leader went. Damn, they'd missed him again.

9

They led the three spare horses back to camp. So far they'd done in four of his men and collected five horses and saddles. Tuey wanted to chase him, but Slocum called her off.

"We better get back and see about Linda and the others. Besides, to chase him is what he wants. That could get us both ambushed."

Tuey looked back with hatred in her diamond eyes. "The Comanches should have cut his throat instead of his sac."

"Been somebody else taken that place. Greed breeds evil and there will always be someone wants someone else's stuff at any price."

"He is worse than they would be."

"Guess we'll never know."

She laughed. "I was raised up to believe there should be no evil."

"You'll have to shoot a lot more outlaws to get there." The extra firearms and holsters hung over his saddle horn. "Shame that one broke that rifle scope when he fell off his horse."

"It has iron sights and we have cartridges."

"May need it," Slocum said over his shoulder and

reined up the dun for her to pull up alongside him leading the three extra horses.

"I want the one that he rode," she said. "He's some horse."

Slocum looked over the broad-chested mountain horse she meant. The deep chestnut was a solid-looking horse. Shorter legged than he liked but sure enough a dandy mount.

"Well, I say you can have him."

Tuey smiled. "I could almost live in these mountains with you."

"Be fun, but you're taking your gold and going back to San Carlos and spit at all those squaws who hated you."

She wrinkled her nose. "Sometimes I wonder how much fun that will be."

"Lots of fun." He threw his head back and laughed. "I can see that Indian in those formal clothes driving you."

"By gawd, I am going to do it."

"Looks quiet enough in camp," he said as they came out to the edge of the timber and could see the cabin.

"You didn't know those two dead men?"

He shook his head. "Never saw them before. One was Julio something and the other had a letter to Tray Shiner."

"That was the gringo who had the rifle."

"Some kind of a remittance man, I think."

"What's that?"

"In countries overseas, the eldest son inherits the estate. The rest, if the family has money enough, are sent away and paid money in an allowance. Lots of them in the west. I don't know about Mexico."

"Oh, yes. Paul Van Blunt is one of them."

"Don't know him."

"He lives in the mountains and comes by to see me for a toss in the bed about the fifteenth of every month. I guess when he gets his money." Tuey laughed.

"They won't have to send Shiner money anymore."

"We should have shot Cicatrize." Tuey looked back with disgust on her dusky face.

"I couldn't get a shot at him."

"Neither could I." She dropped heavily out of the saddle and Mucho came out to help her with the extra horses.

Linda came to the door and frowned. "We'll need more horse feed at this rate."

Slocum waved off her concern. "Any signs of anyone being here?"

"Yes, inside here and in the mine, according to Vargas."

"What's he doing?" Slocum looked around for the man.

"Guarded us while we unloaded mules," Linda said. "Then he went in the mine."

Slocum looked at her hard. "He up to no good in there?"

She gave him a private head shake to discourage his concern and he realized she wasn't worried about Vargas in the mine. Must mean something else. He'd have to keep on the lookout.

"Come in, we have coffee."

"I'll put up your horse," Pearl said, coming out, and took the reins.

"I need to rub him down so he ain't stiff in the morning."

"Ha, I can out-rub you any day." They both laughed.

He followed Linda inside. The interior was floured with mine dust, and rough-hewn—a man's camp. He wondered how long before the women changed that atmosphere.

He settled on a bench and Linda brought him coffee. Mucho was busy flinging water on the floor to keep down the dust. He settled with his back to the thick table and blew on the brew.

"I didn't tell Vargas, but there is no gold vein in the mine. Mucho and I already checked on the trapdoor in the bedroom. That is the tunnel that has the lode in it."

Slocum nodded, then dared to sip the hot coffee.

"Ray figured out long ago," Linda began in a lowered

voice, "that he could not leave a mine unless he concealed the entrance. The ones spying on him all thought he was working the old mine. Shafts go everywhere, but they lost that vein years ago and all the work in the old mine did was produce more tunnels."

"Wonder what Vargas is finding?"

"Who cares, let him look. His true nature, I think, showed, when he didn't help them unload."

"Watch him. He is still a deadly sidewinder."

"I will."

"What do we do next?"

"You want to go look at the gold?"

"Sure." He set down the cup.

"Mucho, make sure that Vargas doesn't find out where we are."

"*Sí,*" the woman said, still wetting down the floor.

The trapdoor was concealed under a blanket, but Slocum saw where they had used a shovel to uncover it. Linda held a candle and began the descend down the ladder into the hole. Mucho nodded to him; she was prepared to restore the door.

When both he and Linda were on the floor of the tunnel, they waved to Mucho and she closed the lid. Linda took the lead. Slocum followed, smelling the dank air. The lamp's light reflected off the walls and wisps of loose dirt seeped down from the timbering. A hundred feet in they came to a room and Linda held the lamp high enough so he could whistle at the sight of the two-inch seam of yellow glow.

"That's some vein."

"See the sacks." She indicated the bulging canvas bags sitting around. "They're full of gold."

"We didn't bring enough mules."

She smiled. "There is plenty here for all of us if someone does not get greedy."

More dirt began to seep down from the timbered ceiling. The rock floor underneath them began to tremble.

"Earthquake," Slocum said. "We better get out of here." They rushed through the tunnel chocked with the billowing dust. Linda handed him the lamp and scrambled up the ladder to the trapdoor. She rapped twice; her face looked blanched in the dingy light. She tried again.

"Why doesn't Mucho answer me?"

"I don't know. Let me up there. Maybe I can force it open—" More rumblings and their world shook like a flimsy box. The air grew harder to breathe.

Linda stifled a scream, hurried down and let him up the ladder. Slocum pushed with both hands. The door gave a little, but did not open. He would need his shoulder against it. Two steps up and he put his upper body to the wood. His knees began to unfold with the effort.

"Oh. Mother of God . . ." She began to pray.

The rung broke and the next one, too. Linda screamed and then began shouting for Mucho. Without those two steps, there was no way that he could ever get enough force to raise the weighted-down trapdoor to open.

"What will we do?" She broke off, coughing on the thick atmosphere.

He undid his bandanna and tied it over her face. "We'll figure out something. Sit down on the ground. Don't exert yourself."

The lamp went out. Damn, was the air that bad?

He settled down with his butt on the rock floor. With her in his arms, they waited—either for the end or Mucho to open the trapdoor. Time went by slowly. Slocum found lots to think about. How he came to the Madras seeking some kind of fun time. Ended up in a damn mine full of breath-choking dust, a fortune in gold, with a beautiful woman in his arms, staring death in the pitch darkness right in the eye.

Then above him a shaft of light began to fill the exit.

"Slocum? Linda? You all right?" Mucho hissed.

"Close enough," he managed and began coughing. He

led the sobbing Linda to the ladder. "I'll—I'll boost you when we get up there. Go ahead."

"What if the ladder breaks again?"

"We'll fall down, but that's better than dying down here. Go."

Once they reached the broken rungs, he boosted her up through the hole. Then the two women hoisted him up until he could belly over the framed doorway.

"I'll make it."

"What—" Linda fell into a fit of coughing.

Mucho bent over her, holding her around the waist and looking concerned at her friend's condition. Slocum, on his knees coughing up the acrid-tasting mud, shook his head.

"What else is wrong?"

"Vargas is trapped in a mine cave-in. I was so afraid you were, too."

"What next?" He tried to clear his numb brain and looked around. "The other two in there now?"

"Yes, but lots of rocks have fallen." Mucho showed her fears in a sad-looking head shake. "Maybe you can help them."

"I'll go see. Get her outside in the fresh air." He motioned to Linda on her knees, gagging on the dust in her throat.

"Take a light," Mucho said. "Candles on the table."

He took one in passing. Maybe someone needed to burn some candles at a shrine for their safety. Especially for Vargas if he was trapped very deep in there and all Slocum had were some women to help rescue him.

Outside, he looked around for any signs of Cicatrize and his bunch. Then he stopped. Across the canyon and high above them, a fresh landslide had buried a goodly portion of the trail across the old slide area. He ran his index finger and calloused palm over his beard-stubbled face. A mine collapse might not be their only problem. He hurried on to see about Vargas and his predicament.

"Take care of her and I'll go see about them."

10

Sweat ran off the end of Slocum's nose; the salt secretions stung his eyes. He bent over, chucking rocks in the small hopper car with Mucho working beside him, grunting and groaning. When it was full, they stood back straddle-legged to catch their breath in the dust-filled air of the tunnel. Tuey drove the mule for the entrance far around the corner from them.

Slocum used his kerchief to mop Mucho's muddy face. His breathing recovering. Linda and Pearl were posted to keep their eyes out. Besides, only two could work in the narrow space and toss the rocks that choked the mine into the mine cart. The sound of the iron wheels screeching on the gritty tracks made his teeth hurt. The two quivering candles on the wall threw big shadows of the two.

"I thought being a *puta* was hard work. My back would ache after a busy night, but this is real work." She pressed on her hips with both hands and made a face.

"That's why you want to be sure there's gold in there to do all this work."

"I hope that Vargas is still alive when we find him."

"Be a big waste if he ain't."

"Mother of God, I thought the whole world was falling in when it began to shake."

"Did you see the new slide over there?"

"Oh, yes. Whew—this is much work."

"Want to trade places with one of the others?"

She made a face to dismiss his concern. "Tuey is coming back."

He could hear the cart rolling free. The Apache had to hand push the cart back. No place to turn her mule and get around the cart in the narrow way. Once she was back there, she turned him around and hitched him for the pull out.

"I have water," Tuey said and handed the water bag back to them.

He let Mucho go first. He wanted more than anything else to get rid of the acrid taste from all the dust he'd consumed. The flavor permeated his nose, throat and mouth, rode like slime on his tongue; even rinsing and spitting didn't help. The biting smell had branded his brain the past few hours.

Back to work, more sharp edged rock to pile in the cart and dump. He wondered if Vargas was even alive under all this. They would need timbers to replace the fallen one if they went very far. Never mind, just work. Load, bend, pick up and do it again. Muscles in his back complained and his fingers felt raw from the sharpness of the debris. The job would take hours, even days.

Linda brought them supper and the two sprawled on the ground and shook their heads in weariness to eat. Mucho's black hair looked ghostly gray and her face powdered white like a Japanese geisha. When she moved her lips, she looked like they were behind a mask.

Slocum wiped his right hand on his filthy pants and looked at it. What was the use? He picked up the burrito off the plate she handed him and saliva filled his mouth. The first bite was no disappointment.

"We are watching close and have seen nothing of him or

any of his men," Linda said, squatting beside him.

"Don't let down your guard. We've killed several of his men. He'll want revenge." He took another bite and chewed slow before he went on. "He knows there's gold here. We won't get out of here short of a miracle without a confrontation."

"He can choose the time and place?"

"Right. We have be to ready all the time for him. Good food."

"Yes. Good food," Mucho said and nodded between feeding her mouth, the effort making granules fall off of her hair. She closed her eyes, as if wary of the whole thing.

"How long will you work here?" Linda asked.

"Long as we can. He's alive in there, we need to save him."

"But could he be?"

"Mines do strange things. Some tunnels only collapse for short distances when the mountains shift. I'm hoping that's all this is."

Mucho turned her ear and listened. She jumped up. "You hear him?"

Slocum nodded. "Vargas, take it easy. We want you out, but not the whole mountain down on us. Can you hear me?"

"Gracias! Gracias!"

"Forget the cart. We need to see if we can make him a passageway out of there."

The threesome began working shoulder to shoulder, pitching rocks back like burrowing groundhogs did dirt.

"There's his hand!" Mucho shouted at the sight of Vargas reaching through. She gasped with excitement.

More and more dust sifted down on them. The continual falling dirt worried Slocum. No timbers to secure it, it could go any minute. Not certain what to do about the problem, but try to make a small orifice. A way that Vargas could crawl through and get the hell out of there.

After thirty minutes of hand digging and tossing aside

chunks of rocks he could see the man's dirty face. Eyes wide and his nose drifted high with dust. A trapped-looking animal, anxious to bolt through and be with them.

Slocum paused, wiped his face on his gritty sleeve and studied the keystone-like effect of the rocks they'd left in place. If the downward pressure of tons of mountain could be supported long enough, then Vargas could crawl through when they made the hole a little bigger. Both he and Vargas removed stones from the base of the opening. With care, Slocum worked another out of the puzzlework and tossed it aside when the bridge held.

"Can you crawl through there?"

"It is narrow."

"I'm afraid much more and the whole thing will fall in."

"Hurry, gawdamnit!" Mucho swore. "I can't stand the suspense no more."

Slocum took his hands and began to pull the man. He hung up on his hips. Both women were trying to pull him, so he would come through the small ring.

"Suck in your ass!" Mucho shouted with impatience.

"I can my belly, but my ass I am squeezing so tight—" Vargas strained and Slocum pulled.

He knew the sharp edges were cutting into the man. But cuts were nothing compared to dying in a mine.

"He's coming!" Mucho shouted.

"My pants!" he shouted.

"We've seen your ass before. Shut up and wiggle."

"*Ai!* Now you are tearing my dick off!"

"Shut up and wiggle, you want to live or you want to screw?"

Slocum was laughing so hard, he about fell down. Then he did fall on his butt when Vargas came out of the hole and spilled on the rocks at his feet. The man was yowling like a hurt tomcat holding his crotch.

Mucho took a light, went over and demanded to see the

damage. After inspecting it, she shook her head in disapproval. "If you had a real dick you might have been in trouble. Such a small scratch on such a small dick, you aren't hurt."

He was hopping around trying to get his pants back on, while Linda was pulling through the hole. "Here."

"Oh, my God. I was almost castrated and she has no sympathy for me." He hurriedly pulled them on.

"I say you owe all of us a big thanks," Linda said. "Instead of bitching. We could have left your ass in there."

Slocum had his arm over Mucho's shoulder and they were headed down the track.

"I need a real bath."

She bumped her hip to his leg as they went up the narrow tracks. "Gringo, I need that and a real good toss in the bed after that. You got that left in you?"

"Maybe."

"Good, 'cause I've been waiting for you." Mucho threw her arm around his waist and hugged him.

"Is he all right?" Pearl asked, meeting them at the entrance, holding the rifle.

"Fine, except he cut his dick off on a sharp rock coming out of the hole," Mucho teased her.

"Lost it all?" Pearl peered in the dark tunnel for the others they could hear coming.

"Cut it off at his belly."

Pearl giggled. "It wasn't very big anyhow."

They all three laughed.

11

Water soaked into his every pore. The long-handled brush that Mucho used on his back felt like a thousand tiny fingers prying out bits of sand from his skin. Her lathered white hands worked over his privates when he stood up and sheets of water ran off him. Molding in and out, she worked with diligence, grinning big up at him. Her fingers gently squeezed the left one that had ached in a cramp for the past hour.

He settled down in the water and took a swig from the mescal bottle that Linda found hidden in the cabin. The liquor was helping ease his back or he didn't give a damn about the stiffness. One or the other, made no difference, relief was all he asked.

Mucho rose up. Her full brown breasts dripping water, she came on her knees through the tank toward him and took his face in her hands to kiss him. The power of her lips and hot tongue in his mouth began to poke needles into the sides of his butt. His shaft began to rise and he took her in his arms to taste more of the honey in her mouth. The stone ache in his left testicle grew more painful. His hips wanted to bury him inside of her. He swept her up in his arms and carried her to the hammock, which overlooked the deep canyon, in the pearly light.

After a perilous swing or two, he parted her short legs and moved between them. She lifted her knees and spread them apart for his entry. A small gasp of pleasure came from her mouth when he went through the gates. His pumping went deeper and deeper until he found the bottom and she pulled his face down to kiss him.

The wild ride began, him hunching it to her and her raising up each time for all of it. Body fluids began to flow and her muscles began to contract around his fiery sword, which tingled with electricity with every plunge. His pubic bone smashed against hers. Her legs split wide, he in as deep as he could go and pounding for more.

Her moaning grew louder and he wondered if the others might not come outside to see about the commotion. She was so into it, she was flopping like a fish out of water underneath him. Her "yes" came with each thrust and soon he began to feel the burning sensation start in his sac. He knew the explosion might blast the end off the head of his dick.

Unable to hold it back, he blew up, felt the needles strike his butt and the depleting forces drain all the strength from his body. They slept in each other's arms.

12

"We've got company." Tuey dismounted the horse and looked back over her shoulder at the mountain.

"Cicatrize back?"

"Three riders on horseback. I hurried back. They're coming up the slope."

"That bastard is coming back?" Vargas moaned. He had come outside and shook his head. "I thought we killed enough of his men, he would leave us alone."

"Linda," Slocum called back to the cabin.

She appeared in the doorway. "Yes?"

"Get everything ready to move out of here. There'll be more quakes. They usually keep shaking for a while."

"Take what we have?"

"I think so if you can get back to it. Don't take any chances."

"What will you do?"

"Go see if I can stop these men. Vargas, you get the mules saddled. I want to be ready to leave here in a few hours and be over the far ridge by dark."

"We'll be ready," Linda said.

"Why me? I could go help you," Vargas pleaded. "What

about the gold? How will we get it out of that mine now that it is caved in?"

"Just saddle the mules. Tuey, grab a bit to eat and we'll go back and see who they are—" The ground began to tremble under him and he nodded at the wide-eyed pair as they searched around. Dirt began to slide off the hillside above the old mine entrance.

"That's what I mean," he said. "Vargas, get those damn mules ready."

"*Sí*. We better hurry," he said as if impressed by the aftershock into a new industrious streak.

Tuey bounded back on her stout horse. "Let's go."

Slocum finished saddling his own and drew up the cinch. In seconds he and Tuey flew out of the compound area and headed for the timber, her leading the way. In a flash, they were riding through the cover of the pines.

"You think there will be more of the ground shakes?" she asked, putting her hard-breathing horse in beside him when they reined to a walk.

"Once they start, sometimes they are hard to shut off."

"I don't like them. Bad things." She swept the hair back from her face. "We go back, will we have much gold?"

"Yes. Enough for you to go back to San Carlos in style."

"I'm going to do that—spit on all of them."

Slocum laughed, then stood in the stirrup and looked toward the crest. "Where do you reckon they're at?"

"They maybe still coming."

"Good. Maybe we can ambush them?"

"Good plan," she said and booted her pony into a trot. "We can set up on the top."

Near the head of the canyon, she pointed to a small pass between two house-sized rocks. If they came over the ridge, they needed to pass through there to get man or beast by that point. She slipped from her pony and took his reins.

"I'll put our horses off in the brush."

He agreed, wondering how far away they were at that point. He jerked the long gun out of the saddle scabbard, then nodded for her to go ahead. On the steep trail, he fought his way up the hillside for the crown. Finally, he was at last bellied down, looking for any sign in the deep canyon on the western slope. A fresh wind swept his face and he could hear the click of their hooves underneath him.

They would be in sight soon. Then he heard her soft footfalls, turned, and motioned for her to join him.

"You can hear them?" she asked.

"Yes, three horses." She made a distasteful face, bellying down with her Winchester to settle beside him in the short grass.

"How many men does Cicatrize have?"

"Who knows? They're all tough and mean as he is."

Slocum nodded he'd heard her. Then in the clearing below them three men rode out of the pines. They wore high-crowned Mexican hats and crisscross bandoliers. *Pistoleros.* The kind of guards that rode for hacienda owners. If they worked for Cicatrize, his caliber of help had gone up a notch.

"You know them?" he whispered to her.

She shook her head. "Tough-looking bastards."

In the next few minutes, Slocum needed to decide, did these three live or die? It was him and the girls against the world up there. He considered Vargas a windbag and not much help when the chips were down.

"What do we do?" she asked, drawing a bead on them with her rifle.

"Send them to hell, I guess."

All she needed. Her rifle belched death and the last rider pitched off his horse—hit hard. Number two reined his horse up and—his mistake. Slocum's bullet hit him in the center of the chest and he slumped off his saddle. The lead man was slinging lead at them. Definitely, but they were out of his range. Her second shot must have creased his horse for he went to bucking like a runaway goat. Slocum couldn't hold him in his iron sights. He quickly fired two more rounds after him, but the gunman was already in the scrub pines.

They could hear him shouting at his horse and must have gotten him under control. Retreating hooves told them that one was riding out and leaving his two compadres to the buzzards. Slocum laid his hand on her to stay there for a moment.

"What do you think?" she asked with a frown.

"They could be bait." He hated that the third one had escaped, but they'd done the best they could.

"Oh, yes." A knowing smile crossed her dark lips. "Now you are thinking like him."

"Yes, I've heard about him. He's tricky."

Some mountain jays called and a nosy raven swept down to sit in a pinyon tree to look over the two still bodies. Both of their horses grazed nearby. Slocum and she remained in their place on the ground—waiting. Rifles in hand, seconds dragged by. Then minutes. Slocum turned his ear to the wind. Nothing. After a half hour of watching the two men's horses for any sign from them, he nodded to her, it was clear. They rose and went for their mounts.

"Should we go get their horses?" Tuey asked when she was in the saddle.

"Yes, guns and ammo, too."

"Too easy," she said and they trotted their ponies.

"He must have had a purpose for them. They didn't expect any trouble, the way they rode in."

"Now Cicatrize can worry."

"How's that?" Slocum dismounted and removed the bandoliers off the first dead man. The outlaw's eyes were open forever. When Slocum hooked the belts over his saddle horn, he decided the shiny cartridges in the loops were new.

"This one has a new pistol, too," she said, stripping the other one of his arms and ammo.

Slocum looked off to the southwest. "Wish I knew his plans for these men. He may have only wanted to see what we'd do."

"Probably to spy on us. What now?"

"Bring those horses on. We need to get the hell out of here. I've got an itch on the back of my neck." He couldn't explain the crawly feeling, but it was there. In a sweep, he was back up in the saddle and they short loped for the mine.

"We heard shots a while ago?" Mucho came running to meet them with her full skirt in both hands.

"Two dead ones. One got away."

Mucho nodded thoughtfully. "Linda is getting the gold out. Vargas is about beside himself over how much there is."

"He better not try anything. I'd be short on patience."

"I will watch him."

"Good, Tuey and I want to ride over and see how bad the slide hurt the trail."

A rumbling grew louder. Both of the women's faces grew paler.

"More earthquakes," Mucho gasped and turned toward the house.

Slocum needed no words; he set out on foot for the cabin. Linda was down in the small mine getting gold out. Inside the open doorway a cloud of thick dust filled the room. Both Pearl and Vargas were coughing.

"Where's Linda?"

"Down there." Pearl, fighting for her breath, pointed at the floor.

Slocum undid his bandanna and used it for a mask. He reached the top of the ladder; not seeing her, he bounded down the new rungs. No light. He wondered where she might be in the inky tunnel.

"Linda! Linda!" He felt his way, tripping over sacks he suspected were gold-filled, brought up to the front for removal.

How far back had she gone? His hands touching the post for the timbering and wall, he made his way back in the tunnel.

"Linda? You back here?"

No answer. He wondered if she had been caught in a cave-in. Then he half stumbled on a body. On his knees, he felt for her.

"You alive, girl?" No reply. He listened to her breath in his ear.

Good, she was still breathing. Must have been hit by a falling rock. He put his arms under her and lifted her up. She made a groan and he smiled.

"We'll be out in the sunlight in a short while," he said softly to her.

"Oh, my head," she moaned. "What happened?"

"Another quake. You must have hit your head on something."

"When will they be over?"

"Soon I hope. Lord, I don't know, girl. We need to get out of here. Tuey and I shot two more of his men. One got away."

"Who were they? You can put me down, I'll be fine."

He could see the ring of light coming from the cabin ahead. "I can pack you to there. Rest a minute."

"Those men you shot—" Choking broke her off.

He shifted her weight in his arms and went on for the ladder he could make out in the dust-filled air. "Looked like most *pistoleros*. We couldn't take a chance on them."

"I thought he might give up."

"No, he's not liable to do that. You have the gold and he wants it."

"How will we ever get back safely?"

"It won't be easy." Slocum didn't want to tell her there would be no safe place as long as Cicatrize was alive.

"Could we buy him off do you think?"

"No way. He wants it all and the more men he loses the more I am convinced he doesn't care about them."

She nodded, then she answered Pearl, asking how she was from above. "I'm fine. Give us a light."

"Coming," Vargas said and came down the ladder with one. "Did it cave in the tunnel?"

"We don't know," Linda said. "You pack these sacks up the ladder."

"Oh, *sí,* I just wondered."

"We about have them all up here. Slocum and I can get the rest."

"Oh, *sí.*"

She took the lamp and started past Slocum, making a private look of disgust at him about Vargas.

"It was threatening to come down. The ceiling back there." She stepped gingerly over some dislodged rocks in the pathway. "How he ever got this tunnel built without a dump cart and track I'll never know."

"He had to haul it out buckets at a time."

"Lots of work."

"There's the cave-in." She pointed ahead toward the jumble of rocks and dirt blocking their way.

"How much more is back there?"

She shook her head. "A few sacks is all."

"We'll leave them and take what we have. Is there enough to make the four of you very rich?"

"Heavens, yes and you, too. None of us will have to lie on our backs and screw some dirty old bastard ever again."

"Good, let's go home."

"What will you do after this is all over?"

"Prop my feet up, get a good place to sit and watch the pretty girls dance."

She shook her head and smiled at him. "You don't give a damn about all this gold, do you?"

"If I have a good horse, some good liquor to drink and a friendly señorita, I'm completely happy."

"And no bounty man looking for you?" She turned and looked for his answer.

"All of that, Linda."

She shook her head as if amused and they started back.

"No more gold?" Vargas asked.

"No, Slocum said that's all there is," Linda told him with a shove.

"But-but—there must be a fortune left back there." He searched into the tunnel at their backs. "You can't leave it here—why Cicatrize will get it—why—"

"If he gets it then we may get away. Our lives are worth more than gold," Linda said.

"Mother of God! You would walk away from a king's ransom?"

"You can stay and have it then," Linda said.

"But—but, I would have no one to guard the place if I mined it."

"Decide," Linda said. "Stay here and look for it or go with us. We are leaving in thirty minutes." She turned with a questioning look at Slocum.

"Thirty minutes," he said softly.

"But—but—"

"You decide," Slocum said, taking up the ladder with a bag of gold on his shoulder.

"Vargas, get those last bags up here," Pearl said, sounding out of her patience with him.

Slocum carried the heavy sack through the cabin out to Mucho, who supervised the packing.

"Save some place for the food and things we will need," he told her.

"I'm using those two new horses for that." Mucho pointed to the two, hitched and standing hipshot.

"Thanks for thinking about that." The sack in the pannier, he brushed his sleeves off and followed Linda to the well. He joined her and washed his face and hands. "You girls have done well this morning."

She handed him the sack towel. "How many days to get back?"

"Three long ones."

"Today won't count since its midmorning now?"

"It'll take three more by my calculations." He studied the quarter-mile-wide fresh earth and rock slide that covered their trail. That might be the toughest thing they faced besides the outlaws.

"We better signal for Tuey to come in," he said. No telling how this would work.

13

The dun horse picked his way gingerly. Slocum was almost to the slide area and wondered how his pony would make the crossover. He glanced at the high walls that surrounded them. On his right, the world pitched off in a sheer down-hill to the boulders over a quarter mile beneath him. Nei-ther horse nor man would survive that fall once he started off it.

He reined the dun uphill when the trail was jammed with waist-high rock and dirt. In short cat-hops, it jumped up the bank and began to veer toward crossing above where the old one went through. Boulders to dodge, real loose fill that gave and stopped the dun up short. Then the agile buff-colored pony retracked and started again. The going was slow, but Slocum wanted tracks the others could safely follow and get across.

The dun lost a hind hoof in a slide, recovered in a catch-up scramble. Reining him up, Slocum looked hard at the bottom underneath him. His heart regained its pace; they went on.

Then he stopped and considered his next move. Seventy or so feet wide of freshly cracked rocks lay ahead. It looked like a prickly place to make horses cross over; he could see nothing, but steeper slopes above and below him. Somehow he needed a path through this rock spill.

He dismounted and began to look for a place he could walk and the horse, too. His boot went down in a crevice and he had to pull it out. This would never work; they'd break some of the animals' legs getting over the obstacle. With none to spare, he tried to see if they could get above it. Actually, the rock spill was in its own depression on the hillside and the slope above it was too sheer.

"We need a shovel and some baskets," Tuey said, standing on her toes, looking at the proposed pathway.

"We'll be hours doing it. But you're right."

"Mules can graze. I'll leave some to watch and guard them," she said and took off at a run.

Slocum found a place close by where the dun could stand hipshot and wait for the outcome. Work soon began. Slocum used rocks to fill in holes and make the pathway. Vargas worked the shovel in the fill, making a path, Linda, Pearl and Mucho carried the half-full sacks on their backs for him to pour out the dirt and stomp it in firm enough to make the way.

It surprised Slocum how fast they filled in the narrow track. Some places his rocks did the trick; others had to be filled in. Crude road-building, he called it. In an hour, they had the path made and the one going back for them much improved.

Mucho ran back to get the animals, while Slocum rode the last hundred fifty feet to the old trail again.

"Hurrah!" Linda shouted and smiled big at him.

Grumpy and acting all done in, Vargas came over on foot, shouldering the short-handled spade. "Better not be many more like this crossing."

Slocum never bothered to answer the man. He stared at the cabin tucked deep on the far side. Would it be there for another trip to the mine? If the earthquakes kept up they might swallow the whole thing. He knew after the last few days that Ray had worked too damn hard up there to end up being shot by bandits. He still owed them for that deed.

"Mount up, we're burning daylight," Slocum said, anxious to put more distance between the mine and them before nightfall. They had a small advantage—Cicatrize would be more cautious coming over the ridge after they'd taken out several of his men up there. Slocum hoped that would be his advantage the first day. Maybe he would remain at the mine and look for the gold. But somewhere in the pit of his burning stomach, his real gut feeling was the bandit leader would be hot on their tracks in less than a day.

"You feel better about it now?" Linda asked, riding up on her bay beside his right stirrup

Slocum looked off at the azure sky beyond the pine boughs over the trail and laughed. "I do. Some things you dread the worst, never happen."

"They work like that. Tuey wants to go back and watch for them."

"Tell her to be careful. We need her."

"I will. If anyone can spy on them she can."

He agreed and watched Linda turn her horse out to go back down the line. Next problem for him was finding enough water for all of them, horses and humans. Twisted in the saddle, he observed Vargas was leading the string of mules. Mucho and Pearl were driving them with quirts when they slacked up. The trotting would help them make some more miles. He booted the dun to go a little faster.

He led them into a large meadow. The first loud bray from one of the jackasses upset a small herd of mule deer that threw their heads up and went bounding away. Best thing about the deers' presence, they had the place to themselves so far, Slocum decided, or the deer would have been gone before they got there. The small stream that fed it looked full enough to water man and beast.

"Here's where we camp," he shouted and the crew looked ready to quit.

Linda rode up and dismounted where he was watering the dun.

"We come far enough today?"

"Far as we could."

"It isn't sundown yet."

He shook his head and smiled at her. "Boss, the next water is four hours' ride north of here."

With a twinkle in her eye, she grinned. "You keep promising me things and you run off with other women."

"I did that?"

She punched him playfully in the gut. "When's my turn?"

He looked around as if searching for something, then shook his head. "Hell it ain't even dark yet."

"I can wait a short while," she said like a sly fox and started leading her horse to where they were unpacking.

"I better look around," he said, stepping back on the dun. "Tell them small fires and not many."

"Yes sir. Don't forget me," she said.

He touched his hat brim and agreed not to forget her, riding off. Lots of woman under that skirt and blouse. Since the first time he met her, he wondered what she would look like in the all together. Something about her— maybe more educated than the others, they all looked up to her a lot for her leadership. Several times on the trip, she had separated the girls before their Latin tempers flared and she did it with ease. Maybe Ray saw that quality in her, too.

Slocum headed up the slope for his look-see. He wondered about Tuey and her scouting efforts, be a lot easier on him if she was there and could read the signs and tracks, if there were any. He sure didn't see all that the half-Apache girl saw in a mere scuff mark. Watching a magpie flit from limb to limb ahead of him, he rode up the steep hillside to better view things.

Seated at last on the ground, he stretched out his looking

glass and began to scan the country beyond the camp. He
spotted a black bear making her way up the south slope
with a roly-poly young cub tagging along behind her. The
antics of the baby bear reminded him of a bold child teas-
ing his mother, but obviously it turned well disciplined
when she threatened to go after him.

Nothing looked out of place. He rose and considered the
higher peaks above them. Two days hard riding and they'd
be in Sierra Estria. Though he did not consider that the
safest place to be with the amount of gold the girls had on
those mules. Perhaps in Magdellania or Hermosillia where
there were secure banks to store it in. Though his experiences with Mexican banks were not the best even with
vaults and guards. The telescope collapsed, he put it back
in the saddlebags.

The business of finding a "safe bank" might sure make
changes in their plans. There would be some desert to
cross, too. Word in this land spread faster than a heliograph
that General Miles put all over the mountains trying to
catch Geronimo. Musing about the military's exercise in
futility, he smiled. Slocum could not recall a thing they did,
but keep the soldiers in touch with each other. Apaches
could do more with mirrors than all of Miles's expensive
setups.

Slocum felt like Tom Horn did about the general—
don't ever give a damn enlisted man a generalship. That
was the Army joke. First thing Miles did was fire all the
Apache scouts and brought in Pimas, Papagos and some
others who couldn't have tracked an elephant in sand. He
learned, too—

Still thinking about his days with the Apache scouts, he
thought about all the nights he spent in the Madras and
wished for any Mucho or Pearl or Tuey or Linda to crawl
in the covers with him. Whew, long nights. Then after all
that hard work, the damn Army beef contractor got Geronimo drunk and he ran off. He heard later the man was paid

a thousand in gold from the Tucson Ring for his trouble. They couldn't afford to lose the hundred thousand soldiers that were in the field down there. Cost Crook his job and Miles came to learn the lessons all over again. And six months later, the ruralists shot the beef contractor who was holding up a stage in Mexico.

He saw Tuey had returned and was squatted by a small fire talking to Linda.

"She saw nothing," Linda said, pouring him some coffee.

"Means nothing." He nodded in thanks to her and she smiled. "We need to talk and I don't need Vargas. Send him off to guard the trail until sundown."

Linda agreed and roused him from his siesta. Slocum watched the coyote tell her, *"Si, mi amiga."* He frowned at Slocum then went for his horse. They waited until he was out of sight and Linda waved them to come over.

"I don't trust Vargas. He maybe harmless, but there is lots of gold on those animals. But that's not here nor there. This gold needs to be in a bank's vault. I've been thinking, if word gets out there will be more bad hombres in Sierra Estria than in prison."

"What should we do?" Mucho said.

"I say, we drop out of the mountains tomorrow and head for Magdellania."

"How many days?" Linda asked.

"Four, maybe five days."

"Bandits?"

He shook his head as if there was nothing he could do about them. "There's bandits anywhere you turn. We move fast, we might get there before the word gets to them."

"I don't want to lose it now that we have it," Pearl spoke up and looked to the others in the red light of the setting sun that bathed the meadow.

"No way," Mucho said. "This gold will free me."

Pearl agreed vocally and Tuey chimed in. "That's the gate to our new world."

"Don't tell Vargas a thing. We'll drop down and then turn west. He can go along or not."

"That's the best idea, everyone agree?" Linda pressed them for their response.

"Yes," came the chorus.

"Beans are ready," Mucho announced, stirring the frothy pot once more with a wooden spoon.

"I'll go get Vargas?" Tuey asked.

Linda approved her mission, then refilled Slocum's coffee cup. He squatted down in deep consideration of the way west. New plans, new destination and no sign of Cicatrize. He blew on the steam. *More miles to cross.*

14

Dawn came into a shadowy world. The sunrise on the far side set the peaks on fire above them. The bray of mules being saddled filled the cold mountain air. Fresh back from making more rounds, Slocum downed his hot coffee as the others loaded the mules. Something woke him in the middle of the night and he'd been on guard most of the rest.

"I came looking for you last night," Linda complained under her breath, dragging a saddle in her right hand past him.

"Sorry, I was out looking for trouble."

She raised her eyebrow in disbelief. "In whose bedroll?"

"No one's. Cross my heart."

"If your rifle hadn't been gone, I'd sure been calling you a liar." She grinned big in understanding and lugged her saddle to the horse.

"Yes ma'am," he said and tipped his hat to her.

No sign of Cicatrize meant nothing except Slocum didn't figure the outlaw could afford to let four women beat him at his own game. This business would soon come down to the principle of it all. Maybe even more important than all of the gold.

Slocum tossed out the contents of his cup, tied it on his saddle and headed for the west side of the meadow.

"Hey," Vargas shouted. "The trail goes north. We can't go that way."

"Don't worry," Pearl shouted. "He knows the way."

"No, no, the trail goes north. You've got to go north here."

"Let Slocum lead, he's got us this far." Linda rode in and told the man firm enough he shut up.

Slocum rubbed his whisker-bristled mouth with his fingertips as he rode in the lead. Why was Vargas so upset about his change in course? Maybe he did have plans of his own for the gold. For that outburst, it would bear watching him closer.

By midmorning he could see the sunbaked land, arid brown grass and cactus sprawling beneath them into the western horizon. They would camp in the desert that night and several more nights before they reached Magdellania.

A hot wind in his face, Slocum rode ahead to find them a place to stay. He found a small ranch and the man agreed for five pesos to feed their animals hay and let them camp there overnight. The matter settled, he rode back to meet his crew.

"Whew," Linda said, wiping her forehead on the back of her hand. "I forgot how hot Mexico was and why I lived in the mountains."

Slocum reined the dun around to track beside her. "You'll be ready to go back, too. I have a place to stay for five pesos and he will feed the animals hay."

"Sounds good. How far ahead?" She looked across the heat-wave-distorted big cactus and mesquite cover for sight of something.

"Maybe an hour."

"Slocum has us a place up ahead to spend the night," she said, twisting in the saddle to let the others know. "About another hour's ride, he says."

"Yeah, his hour or ours?" Pearl teased, riding in to slap a lagging mule.

"Either way," he said.

"I think Vargas is really upset about this route," Linda said under her breath.

"Who cares? No one asked him to come along."

She nodded. "Wonder what he had planned?"

"He planned to jump you girls and take the gold."

"You may be right."

Slocum closed his gritty-feeling eyes and agreed. The day's journey and furnace blast had numbed his mind. He put Vargas on the head of his list of things to watch. No telling what he would try or do; obviously the change in plans and route had him upset.

A little two-bit outlaw was all he was and all he would ever be—if he lived that long. If he tried anything while with the crew, Slocum had a bullet for him.

They rode into the small headquarters, mules braying, the rancher's dogs barking. Tito Callaso was a short, dried-up looking man, sunbaked till his exposed arms, hands and face looked like dark leather. His woman acted shy and remained inside the doorway as if not to expose herself to the noisy bunch taking over her place.

Three of the girls dipped their faces in the horse tank to cool off, while they watered the thirsty mules and horses. The windmill continued to pump a pipe full of water to resupply it. Linda took Slocum aside.

"No one knows we have gold, but us. What if word gets out, like this little cockerel here who acts so fascinated with the girls." Her last words had a cutting edge.

Slocum agreed the man was doing his best to impress the others. "It's up to them. They have as big a stake in this as we do."

Linda looked to the sky for help. "How many more days?"

"Three, I hope."

"I will pray a lot."

"It sure won't hurt." He jerked off his saddle and pads, then sat the saddle so the horn was down and the sheepskin could dry. "We aren't there yet, either. Tell the girls to be quiet. I'll tell Vargas the same."

"I will. Good luck."

Callaso acted as if he had nothing to do but flirt with the girls. He brought an ax and split wood for them when they built a fire. His tales of travels were bold and the girls acted interested as they hurried about fixing the evening meal.

The inevitable question came—what was their purpose in crossing this backcountry? Slocum was squatted down blowing on too hot coffee when he turned his ear to hear the answer.

"We are going to Guaymas and start a big whorehouse," Pearl said. "You want to come along."

"You girls do that?" Callaso asked, looking taken aback.

"We do lots of things," Mucho said, from on her knees at the fire. "But right now we're cooking supper."

They all laughed and he laughed, too. Vargas frowned and squatted down beside Slocum.

"You aren't serious about Guaymas, are you?"

"That's where they said we were going?"

"Pearl said—"

Slocum shook his head and frowned to silence the man. Let them think what they wanted them to—in another day Vargas would realize they weren't going to Guaymas.

The rooster had his arm over Pearl's shoulder when she went to get a pail of water. Vargas made a black face at the sight of them and spoke under his breath. "That little bastard must get horny up here."

"He has a wife," Slocum said.

"Yes, but a wife is your duty. A *puta* is to fuck. Big difference."

"I wouldn't know."

"Why?" Vargas batted his eyes.

"I never had a wife."

They both laughed. Slocum noticed Pearl still wasn't back with the water. Mucho stood and looked off in the inky night for her. Then with a disgusted shake of her head she went back to her cooking.

Linda was making flour tortillas on the grill and the stack grew taller. She used her hands to form them from a small ball of dough. She kept the sheet of iron covered, turning them over with her nimble fingers.

Still no Pearl. Still no water. Tuey was sitting cross-legged on the ground, busy repairing a girth. Slocum wondered when someone would call for her. He wasn't listening to Vargas's rambling. Then Pearl appeared carrying the bucket and grinning. No sign of Callaso. In a little while, he came whistling into camp.

He came over and dropped to his haunches. "How did you two get so lucky?"

"What's that?" Vargas asked him.

"All the pussy you will ever need." He threw his hand out at the girls around the campfire.

"They ain't ours."

"Aw. Come on, you two get it for free."

"I don't. Do you Slocum?"

"No."

"You could have fooled me," Callaso said and shook his head.

"Come eat," Mucho said. "You too, hombre," she said to him.

He tried to back out, but she wouldn't hear of it. He finally surrendered and joined them filling their tin plates from the pots and kettles on the stove.

"Some feast," he said, taking a couple of tortillas. "What will you call your new place?"

"Lightning," Pearl said.

"Why's that?" Collaso asked.

"Because that is all it will take for you to get off in there."

A little red-faced in the firelight, the rancher about choked. "Oh, I see."

After the meal, Slocum took his bedroll on his shoulder and went up on the rise to shake it out. A thousand stars pricked the sky and some of the day's heat was evaporating. How long would it be before someone tried to take the gold? If they were smart they would need it packed up when they tried to take it. Unlike money it would not be easy to sell so much. But there were markets for everything in the world and a price, too.

Seated on his butt, Slocum smoked a small cigar he found in his saddlebags. The nicotine was settling him. A coyote yipped in the night and some bats swooped down after insects. Maybe they would be there in two days. Better get some sleep, morning would come soon enough.

15

"Vargas took a horse and left," Tuey whispered in his ear.

Slocum's eyes flew open. His fist automatically grasped the butt of his Colt under the covers. Then recognizing her in the starlight, he nodded.

"What did he take with him?" he whispered

"You mean did he steal any gold?"

"Yes."

"None. Only the horse and what he had on him. We were all sleeping around the gold."

Slocum nodded and considered going after him. Vargas couldn't be far away. Might be best to let him go and to be rid of him anyway, though he knew the miserable sumbitch was on his way to get more confederates. The ones, he figured, who were waiting for their return to the village to jump them and take all the gold.

It would be hard for Vargas to ride for his help up there and get back on their trail. Still, desperate people did desperate things. They would need to move out. He checked the sky; still a while until daylight broke over the Madras.

"It's cold out here," she said, hugging her arms.

He raised the blanket up and she slithered in under the

covers against him. "Damn, you are warm. How does the desert get so cold at night? We cooked all day in the heat."

"I don't know," he said, sliding his hand under her short dress and caressing the inside of her leg.

"You don't care, either." She laughed and snuggled against him.

By dawn, he was squatted at the fire drinking coffee. The mules were loaded. The absence of Vargas had been observed and discussed.

"That windy bastard. I came along to help you women," Mucho said, squatting by the fire. "Help hell. He's about as much an outlaw as I am a nun. I wish I had been there when Cicatrize gave him his in the butt that time. Bet he screamed like a pig."

The others agreed.

The sleepy-eyed Callaso came down to the camp, tucking in his shirttail. "You already loaded?" He blinked at the sight of the ready mules.

"We've got places to be," Slocum said to him.

"I bet you do." He tossed his too long hair back. "Next time I am in Guaymas, I'll come by your place."

"Oh, do," Pearl said, seated on the ground with her plate in her lap.

"I better get back. I think you make my wife, she is jealous."

"Have a good day," Slocum said and waved at the man's departure.

"Ah, sí, anytime." He hurried back toward the *jacal*.

"What's so funny?" Mucho asked the snickering Pearl, holding her fist to her mouth.

"He—" Unable to contain herself, she laughed out loud then recovered. "Last night, he whipped out his little hard-on down there by the water trough to show me and he got so excited his gun went off."

"You were impressed?" Mucho asked.

"Yes, I never saw one explode so fast in all my life."

"I wondered why you took forever to bring the water back."

"I couldn't. I'd have laughed out loud."

"Never bothered you before." Mucho shook her head, still amused.

"Let's go," Linda said. "Slocum wants to be moving."

The trail grew narrow descending the face of the mountain and the mountain and the day began to warm rapidly. Slocum looked back and wondered how far away Vargas's men were hiding out. And where was Cicatrize? The ambush of his men would not silence him for long. Perhaps it had only made him more convinced to attack them.

Midday, they watered in a small stream in the foothills and prepared to cross the desert. Slocum estimated they were two days or more from their goal. He scoped the mountains and saw no sign of pursuit but, collapsing the scope, knew it made no difference. Not one, but two parties were after them. Who could tell there wasn't more? Word traveled fast and greed was an all-consuming fire.

He pushed them hard and they found some stock water close to the fiery sundown. Too stagnant for human usage, they used their own canteens and the small barrels. A fire quickly blazed and food soon bubbled in the pots.

"How much farther?" Linda asked him as he worked on the partially torn girth.

"Another long day and we should be close enough."

"Have we outrun them?"

He shook his head. "No, we are only ahead of them so far."

"Can that be fixed?" She had squatted down close to him to examine his work.

He looked into her smooth face illuminated by the red light of the fire. "A man made it, another can fix it."

She laughed. "You don't let things depress you for long."

"Life's short at best. One has to make the best of the time he has."

"So strange. You have no yen to settle down and live like normal people?"

"I'm a realist. There is nowhere on earth I can do that. Sooner or later they'd come looking for me."

She nodded she'd heard him. "We are grateful that you've done so much for us. We would have never made it up there, if not for you."

"So far we're doing good. The good Lord gives us two more days and we'll be there."

"Do you think we could ever go back again?"

"To the mine?"

"Yes."

"If there aren't any more earthquakes and some claim jumper hasn't taken it over, you could."

"I think we were lucky to get out with what we did."

Slocum agreed and looked up as Mucho brought him a cup of coffee. Somewhere out in the greasewood and cactus, a coyote howled at the stars. He turned his ear to the soft night wind and listened. Nothing sounded out of place.

16

Predawn, they saddled the stock, loaded the heavy panniers on the cross bucks and with a chorus of mules braying, headed northwest. Against the coolness that settles in the desert before sunup, they wrapped themselves in blankets and rode out through the spiked silhouettes of the tall cacti.

Cold beans wrapped in tortillas were handed out to eat on the way. Everyone felt an urgency, led by him. He wanted the sanctity that Magdellania offered, ruralists' protection and the safety of a town. Men like Vargas avoided such places. Mexican law dealt tough with offenders and few prisoners were ever brought back for incarceration. So remaining in the Madras was much safer for them than to venture out to the populated areas.

Midday, he saw the small village and the church temple. He turned in the saddle to Linda. "We can water our animals at the well in the square. But everyone keep their eyes open." With his arm, he waved Tuey up with them.

"You go ahead. Get on the roof of a building with your rifle and watch close. We'll water the stock in the city trough and then ride on. You see any sign of trouble, you can warn us with a shot."

Tuey nodded and used the stock of her rifle to spank her pony. In a flash she was gone through the spiny forest that surrounded them. A trail of dust spun up by her pony's hooves. When he turned back Linda nodded in approval.

"We making good enough time?"

"Yes, giving them a drink here at midday means we can trot them all this afternoon and get there by sundown."

No sign of Tuey, he held up the train on the last rise and used his telescope. Nothing looked out of place. Her horse stood hipshot behind a cantina. She must be on the roof. They had coverage—good.

"Let's go in," he said and booted the dun for the cluster of adobe buildings on the grassless hillside. The unfinished second tower of the church beside the belfry one stuck above the rest. They never finished churches, so the king could not assess taxes on them when Mexico belonged to Spain.

A few goats and loose burros looked up with curiosity at the train's approach. Some noisy rooster crowed his head off about successfully topping a hen; otherwise the sleepy town looked and sounded like a thousand more sites below the border. Slocum felt tense. He always felt tense going into the unknown—any site where an ambush could occur.

The drum of hooves of his train sounded loud entering between the walls of buildings that surrounded the well in the square. Slocum kept his hand on his gun butt. Then he rode the dun into the square.

Something was wrong. He searched for Tuey on the roof. There was nobody at the well.

"Get out of here!" he shouted and the shocked-faced women wheeled their horses.

The front doors of the church flew open and gunslinging riders burst out on horseback. Across the street, another handful of hombres firing pistols came charging out of the stables. Trap. The square was full of screaming madmen.

Outnumbered and outgunned, he hoped to block the way out until the women and mules could flee.

Slocum took one rider off his horse with a bullet in the chest. The second one he shot point-blank in the face. In the melee, someone hit him from behind with a rifle butt and the world went dark.

An acrid taste of dirt in his mouth, he realized that three men were carrying him somewhere in the dark. He could see stars. His biggest dread was they thought he was dead and planned to bury him.

"Bring him in here," a woman in charge said when they reached the shaft of light coming from a doorway.

"Ah," she said, peering at him as they went along. "You are awake."

"Yes," he managed.

"There, set him on the bed."

"The women?"

"Two are dead."

"There were four."

"Only two dead ones here. One is a breed girl, short."

"Tuey." He felt stabbed.

"The other was a dark-skinned girl."

"Mucho."

"I guess. But we will bury them in the churchyard."

A knot formed behind his tongue and he couldn't swallow. Bastards. The woman in her forties with gray in her hair began to bathe his face with a cloth and water.

"How much gold did they have?" she asked.

"Lots," he managed.

"They had been here since last night. They killed two of our men. Raped several young women. We knew there was nothing here to steal."

"Did he have a scar on his face?"

"Yes. That is Cicatrize." She shook her head in disapproval. "He rapes young boys now."

"Sorry, we didn't bring him here."

"I know, but I hope you find him and kill him."

"I will or die trying."

"And"—she gritted her teeth—"cut off his pecker and bring it to me when you're done with him."

"He rape you?"

"No, my twelve year old."

"Girl?"

Her eyes clouded with raw anger, she shook her head. "I will get you some food. Can you sit up?"

"I think so."

"Help him, Jose," she said sharply and the man rose to obey her.

Slocum held out his hand to stay him. "I'm fine."

"Why only four pretty women?" he asked.

"It was their treasure. I had no time to hire guards. One man ran off, I thought to rob us—but he wasn't with Cicatrize."

"We couldn't warn you."

Slocum nodded that he understood. "I'm grateful for you caring for me, anyway."

"No problem. Will you get an army and go after him?"

"No, I'll go. He can see an army coming."

"You watch for the one looks like a bulldog. He is the one who garroted the breed girl."

Slocum winched. The outlaw had put a garrote around Tuey's neck, then jerked her up behind his back and hung her, either breaking her neck or strangling her to death. The notion made him sick to his stomach.

She brought a tray of food. More than he could ever eat and hot coffee. He sipped it first to let the caffeine clear his brain.

"The other woman?" He glanced over at the gray-bearded Jose.

"They shot her between the buildings, but she gunned down three of his men before they got her. She was holding them off." With a grim shake of his head, he looked with pained eyes at Slocum. "She was fighting like a man."

Mucho had been trying to hold them off. Good enough. What a shame. "I guess that made about five that were shot?"

"Six, and we made sure they were dead." Jose gave him a solemn nod.

"How many men did he have?"

"Lucia?" Jose spoke out to her. "How many *pistoleros* were here in the village?"

"Ten, counting him."

"That means four are left?" Slocum asked, picking up his burrito to take a bite.

"*Sí*, and no one shot the bulldog-looking one that killed the Indian one."

"I'll find that sumbitch." Slocum had his name written down in his mind. *Bulldog one.*

Jose made a quick sign with his hands like to break a chicken's neck.

Slocum agreed. "Did they take my dun horse?"

"No," Jose said. "We are horse poor here now."

"Saddle him and get me one more that looks stout."

"But, señor?"

"I must get after them. The longer I wait, the further away they will be. I want to catch them this side of the Madras."

"Pack him some food," Jose said to his woman, who sat sewing by the fireplace. "I will get his horse and another good one."

"*Gracias.*"

The man rose, nodded to him and headed out the front door.

"You should not ride away in the dark," she scolded Slocum.

"I have to get them."

"Or be killed," she said under her breath.

"You believe in candles in the church."

"*Sí.*"

He gave her a quarter. "Burn some for me, then."

A warm smile crossed her face. "You are a tough man. I thought he would come back and kill you, but he lost so many men he needed all of them to take the pack train back."

"I think you're right."

"We all live to hate the things we left undone," she said and nodded, then lowered her voice. "Cut his dick off at the belly for me."

He nodded when he'd heard her words as she went off to get him food to take along.

"Jose can ride a ways with you and be sure you don't fall out of the saddle," she said, sounding in disapproval of his plans.

"*Gracias,* but I'll ride hard."

"He is plenty tough. But there was nothing we could do. There were so many *pistoleros*. They had no manners. They hid in the church, too." She crossed herself and bowed her head. "God will make them pay. Even took their horses inside the church. They were heretics."

"Six paid with their lives."

She nodded grimly and went to get him some food to take along while he ate. Her cooking tasted fresh and slid down his throat. He washed down his meal with the coffee and nodded when she returned with a cloth sack for him.

"Jerky and some tortillas."

"I'm in your debt. That will be fine. Can I pay you?"

"No. You have to rid the world of such bastards, I would not expect money. Ride with God." She stood on her toes and kissed him on the cheek.

He nodded in acknowledgment and headed for the door.

"I will ride a ways," Jose said, meeting him outside in the starlight.

"Fine." Slocum tied the sack on his horn, checked the cinch and swung up in the saddle. Jose handed him the reins to the second horse. Time to ride away and find them.

"Lead the way," he shouted to Jose and they sped from the village.

17

The faraway outline of the Madras began to give birth to the sunrise. The faint glow turned to purple as the pangs of delivery drew closer. Slocum and Jose rested their horses. The older man dismounted to search for their tracks. His nod was enough to make Slocum feel better. Earlier, the outlaws had ridden through there. No telling if the women were alive or dead.

No matter, they would pay with their lives for what they had done to Tuey and Mucho. Anything else would be heaped on their heads. Torture and a slow death would not be enough for the likes of the killers—Slocum wished for an Apache to string them upside down, one at a time, and boil their brains over a small fire. Their waiting to die would be the longest.

"Do you need to return home?" Slocum asked the man when he remounted.

"If I could be of some help to you, I would go further."

"Yes, you may come, but I won't return to your village until I find them or kill Cicatrize."

"I understand. Maybe I can help you do that."

They rode through the great cactus and across the greasewood flats, occasionally scaring up a tall-eared jackrabbit who only ran to a ridge top then paused to study the invaders. Easy for Slocum to lean over and see the narrow tracks of the mules. They looked to be walking, which encouraged him.

Midday, the heat waves distorted the horizon and a small cloud of dirt told him they were close. He pointed out their dust to Jose.

"Ah, *sí*, we have caught up with them."

"The pack train, anyway."

"You think the bad one is there?"

"If you would like to stay here?"

"Give me a gun. I want to fight them."

"I promised your wife. . . ."

"Ah, señor, I promise her a lot, too." He threw his head back and laughed. Slocum joined him.

"Here. Check the caps are on each nipple, except the empty one under the hammer." He handed the man a small .30 caliber Colt from his saddlebags.

Jose looked the pistol over and nodded in approval. Then he booted his horse out with Slocum into a trot.

"Make them count," Slocum warned him. The man agreed.

Slocum chose a game trail that veered to the right. He wanted to come at them from the side where they least expected an attack. The element of surprise always helped win a battle. The path through the spiny cactus and brush grew narrow. For a while he wondered if he had been mistaken, then they were behind a hog back that separated them from the train. In the sandy draw, he gave a head-toss to make their horses lope and Jose agreed.

The hard-breathing dun between his knees, he felt sure the noise of the mules and the rest would cover the sounds of their fleet travels. At the point of the ridge beside them, he reined up and switched horses. Jerking the Winchester out of the scabbard, he turned to Jose and tossed him the dun's reins.

"I'm going to have a look. You stay here. There's a shot, you can run or come help me."

"I will join you."

"Fair enough. Make those five bullets count."

"I will, señor."

With his heels to the bay horse, he set up the hillside. Cat-hopping, the surefooted mountain pony dodged boulders and spiny plants until a few yards from the top. Slocum swung down and jerked the .44/40 out of the scabbard. The braying of the jackasses sounded like music in his ears. His soles scrambling on the slick gravel, he knelt down and took off his hat. Then he crawled the last two yards to peek down at the train. He counted three men and to his relief saw them with their hands bound to the saddle horn—Linda and Pearl.

He cocked the hammer back and looked down the sights at the outlaw on the roan horse leading the train. The rifle rocked in his hands, belched smoke in his eyes. The rider hit hard, pitched off the horse. Wide-eyed, the mules shied back.

Slocum swung the barrel around, reloaded and sighted on a bearded man under a peaked sombrero fighting to draw his pistol. The rifle roared and the struck *pistolero* squeezed the trigger off, causing his horse to have a fit. No doubt creased or struck by the man's own bullet, the animal, head down, buckling away, cartwheeled into a giant organ cactus, sending his hard-hit rider off into the chaparral. The horse struggled to get up, screaming in pain.

When Slocum whirled to find the last one in his sights, all he could see was the dust of his fleeing horse's heels. Damn, that must have been the one they called Bulldog. On his feet, he began the descent off the steep hillside.

"Oh, thank God!" Linda shouted with a look of relief on her dust-floured face.

Beating her horse with her heels, Pearl came over as he sliced through Linda's bonds. "You are the prettiest man I have ever seen."

"Ever," Linda repeated rubbing her rope-burned wrists while he freed Pearl.

"Where's Cicatrize at?" he asked.

"Rode to get more help this morning," Linda said.

Slocum grimaced. "Bulldog went to warn him, we better make tracks."

Linda's eyes flew open at the approach of another rider. "Who is that?"

"Jose. He's with us. We better round up the mules and head back for his village." The old man brought him his horse. He took the reins and thanked him.

"Can we make it there?" she asked, concerned, remounted on her circling horse.

Slocum mounted his own in one fluid move, nodded to her question. They'd damn sure try to, anyway. Then he saw the older man was busy catching the pack string leader and bringing him back.

"Take them and head for home. Cicatrize's gone to get more men."

"He will need more," Jose said defiantly and rode by him, leading the string of braying mules.

"*Sí, mi amigo.*" Slocum shared a confident look with his helper. "I must kill the horse that fell down. Then I'll catch the other loose one. We can't leave anything."

"Are they both dead?" Jose asked, over his shoulder.

"They will be when the buzzards pluck their eyes out."

"Good enough for them."

"Girls, whip the mules," Slocum shouted and waved for them to get out of there. "We have no time to spare."

He found the injured bay horse standing past the broke-off organ pipe trunk. It was unable to put any weight on its right leg that dangled like a pendulum. Either a broken shoulder or leg. He eased the rifle out and a bullet inches under his pained eye crumbled the animal to the ground. No more suffering. Slocum rode over and found the rider facedown. The red blood from the wound in the center of his back had soaked through the shirt. Let the buzzards have him. He reined his horse for the other loose one.

Dragging his reins, the horse moved sideways and the first pass Slocum missed catching the reins. Forced to boot his pony in close, he caught them. Starting after the others, he heard the distressed call of the first bandit.

He reined up, saw the man half sitting up and reading the red blood in his hand.

"I'm shot. Don't leave me."

"Like you shot those women back there?"

"I swear on my mother's—"

"Swear on anything. This looks like a good day for you to die."

"Mother of God! You can't leave me here alone."

"I'm not. I counted three buzzards coming to see you. Good day." He booted the bay after the disappearing pack train. Lots of miles to cover, and he twisted in the saddle to look at the hazy purple mother mountains. No telling how long that Cicatrize would be getting more men.

He ignored the bandit's screaming protests and hurried to catch the others.

Past midnight, the spent crew rode into Jose's village of Saint Tomas. Mules snorted in the dust with their weariness and people brought lamps to come see about them.

"I wish to buy corn for the mules and horses. Each one must be rubbed down and stabled on soft ground." Slocum dropped heavily from the saddle and handed the reins to someone in the crowd who rushed out to help.

"*Sí*, señor, we will do it." Jose's wife, Lucia, took charge of things. "Go to my house. They will fix you food and a place to sleep.

"Four hours is all we dare sleep. Post guards. Give them my rifles," Slocum told her.

"We will be ready for them."

He nodded woodenly. His head hurt from the hit on the back, but he could see the stock was being unloaded.

His arm in her grasp, she shoved him toward her lighted doorway. "Go and eat and sleep. No one will steal an ounce."

"I will," he mumbled and moved like a dead man toward the house.

"Slocum?" Linda hissed at him. "Are we safe here?"

He nodded. "Safest place I know . . ."

"Good, I am too tired to fight."

He pinched her dust-coated nose and laughed. "So am I."

His eyes refused to open. Glued shut with adobe. He wondered as he sat up and rubbed them with the sides of his fists if they would ever be all right. Time to get up. He could smell good food cooking. A soft predawn light filtered in the room where he'd slept on a pallet. He's slept in his boots and clothing that bore an acrid smell of alkali dust. Squatting beside Linda, he shook her.

"Time to get ready to ride."

She blinked at him in disbelief, then sat up in a coughing fit. At last she managed to nod acceptance of his words. Pearl rose up using the blanket to shield off the morning chill.

"For God's sake, I never thought I'd ever sleep again, but I did." She peeled back the cover and rose. Adjusting the waist of her skirt, she swept the hair from her face and shook her head.

Lucia came in and stood with her hands on her hips, appraising them in the shadowy room. "The village can spare you three men to get you to where you are going."

Linda nodded. "We will give you one of our slain sisters' part of the treasure for everyone."

"That would be generous of you," Lucia said. "How much is that?"

"Maybe twenty thousand pesos," Slocum said quietly.

A small whistle escaped her brown lips. "We could buy a pump and fix the church and . . ."

"Think hard," Slocum said. "The men you send with us to bring back your money must not be greedy men."

Lucia held her forehead and shook her head in dismay. "I knew you had riches out there, but so much?"

"Sorry, but we need to load our mules and ride for Magdellania."

"Oh, yes, excuse me. We have food ready for all of you and the men are preparing the mules."

Slocum herded the two women out into the great room. They took their places at a table set full of bowls of things to eat. The rich aroma caused the pangs of hunger to gnaw at the sidewalls of his guts. Young women rushed about to bring them mugs of coffee and hand them dishes of fruit and meats.

Before him was enough food for an army—these towns-people had no prior knowledge that Linda would bestow such a reward upon them. This village was not a rich place with plenty. From the looks of things, they all had a hard time barely getting by, yet they found it in their heart to treat someone worse off, they figured, than themselves

"Señorita Linda is going to fix the church roof," Lucia announced and held out her hand to the seated woman. "Then she is going buy us a windmill to pump our water, too."

When Slocum looked up from feeding his face, every door and window was filled with excited faces. Heads bobbed around the room in approval, everyone clapping and cheering.

"Jose and two other men will ride with them to Magdel-lania and bring back the pesos."

A buzz went through them. Slocum looked up in time to see the padre come though the crowd in his brown habit.

"Bless you three. Not for what you have promised the people here this morning, but for making us all feel impor-tant. We have worked as a team to help you. It shows what we can do. Perhaps when you ride on, this effort will remain."

"Father, we hope it will," Slocum said and straddled the chair. "We must get to Magdellania. I hope we have not brought trouble to this place and thank all of you."

The priest held up the cross from around his neck and spoke in Latin. They were receiving his blessing. *They might need it, too.*

18

Mules braying, they left Saint Tomas. The priest sprinkled holy water on them as they went by. Each one bore a cross of dust on their spine under the padding and pack saddles. Slocum knew looking over the pack string passing under the arch that they were as blessed as any train could be.

Jose rode at the lead. The other two younger men carried rifles taken from the outlaws and rode on each side. Waving more long guns from the roofs, the men on guard shouted for them to have good luck and return soon.

"How far?" Linda asked, riding in beside him.

"By afternoon we can be there if we hurry."

Linda looked back across the desert behind them, then turned back and patted her horse on the neck. "I wonder if we can do that?"

"I'm planning on that."

"What will you do with your share?"

"I really don't have much use for it."

"You are serious, aren't you?"

"Oh, six weeks from now I'll be broke and wish I had a potful. Guess right now, a hot bath, shave, haircut, some fresh clothes and a bed full of some gorgeous woman would do me for awhile."

"But why?"

"Money would only attract more bounty hunters. I don't need them."

"Maybe you could buy your freedom."

"Gave up on that idea years ago, too."

"When we get all this gold in a bank, Pearl and I plan to buy a hacienda. Will you come by and see us?"

He nodded. "Oh, yes. Make them trot faster," he shouted to the two men. "I want to be there before the bank closes."

"You worried about him?"

"I will till he's dead."

She agreed and booted her horse to make him keep up.

The sun was going down when they entered the busy main street. Dodging burro train vendors that peddled firewood, water, ground corn and food stands with smoky fires, the train also was threatened by expensive phantom carriages with high-stepping horses.

One fancy-dressed man rose from his seat in the carriage and waved them aside. "Get those mules out of my way."

Slocum booted his horse over and looked hard at the man. "You know who that lady is?"

"I have no idea and I don't give a damn."

"Excuse me, señor. What is your name?"

"Renaldo Gilbert."

"And, Señor Gilbert, may I ask who is your banker?"

"My banker." The man frowned and looked with a question at Slocum.

"His name?" He checked the shuffling dun.

"Señor Koehn."

"You owe him money?"

"What business is that of yours?"

"Not mine, sir. But by dark that lady you have treated so rudely here will own your mortgage. Good day."

"But—but you can't."

"What was that about?" Linda asked, scowling back at the man shouting and waving at them.

"We are investing your money in Señor Gilbert's mortgage today."

"Why?"

"Mexican banks don't loan money without lots of collateral. I figure that man owns a hacienda around here and is probably overextended."

"You saw all that looking at him?"

"Where are we going?" Jose asked.

"Señor Koehn's bank."

"That's the big one on the square."

"That's the one," Slocum agreed and winked at her. "Let me do the talking. You girls just listen."

"Hear him?" Linda asked Pearl.

"Damn sure did. I love it."

Armed guards stood beside the iron-gated entrance when Slocum dismounted. He saw the portly head of them come striding over in his pressed tan uniform. "Ah, señor, we expect some of our important customers to drive up here soon. Will you move the mules, please?"

"Will you tell Señor Koehn that a man called Slocum is out here in the street and wishes to speak to him."

"Impossible. He is a very busy man." He shook his head, making it look like his fuse was growing short.

Slocum waved his finger before the man's face. "Then I will have to tell him that you refused to let me deposit a half million dollars in gold in his bank."

"How much?"

Slocum put his arm on the man's shoulder like they were old friends and guided him to the last mule. "Watch his hind feet. He kicks sometimes."

"Ah, *sí.*" The man swallowed hard. "You really have that much gold?"

"Undo the rope and take off the cover." He waved the others back.

"My name's Slocum, what's yours, captain?"

"Mylesta, Gregorio Mylesta." His fingers shook as he completed untying the rope. He dropped it and pulled off the dusty sunbleached canvas. Then swallowing hard again, he unbuckled the straps that held the pannier tops and soon tossed them back. Beads of perspiration ran down his face.

Slocum handed him a knife and for a second he blinked at it. Then woodenly he nodded and cut the cord holding the canvas bag shut. His jaw sagged at the sight of the flakes and nuggets that glittered in the sun light. Quickly he flattened it back.

"My apologies, señor, señoritas." He swept off his cap and bowed to them. "Juan, get all the guards and the employees at once and get them out here. We can't have this in the street any longer. Take the mules inside the gate, señor." He waved for Jose go ahead. "You know this is very dangerous?"

"Been that way for days, Captain." Slocum shared a private look with both women.

They agreed and dismounted, straightening out their skirts and adjusting their blouses.

"Ladies," Slocum said with a bow. "The Grand Bank of Magdellania is now open."

If there had been bees in the vault, nothing could have swarmed more like them than the bank employees did. Both women were escorted to a sitting room and Slocum kept tabs on the unloading process. He was standing in the doorway when a man wearing a monocle and a gray-streaked walrus mustache approached him.

"They call you Slocum?"

"Yes?"

"My name is Herman Koehn."

"I've been looking for you, sir." Slocum shoved out his hand and they shook.

"They tell me you have a considerable amount of raw gold."

"We do, sir. I represent the young ladies inside."

"May I ask where it came from?"

"The Lost Harlot Mine."

The banker made a face. "Never heard of it." He watched the last pannier being carried in by the bank employees.

"Would you send a man with my guards to have their supper?" Slocum asked the man. "I can pay you, but they are unfamiliar with your city. Send them someplace nice. They are hard workers."

"Of course. I will pay the tab, sir. Gregorio, wine and dine his men on me."

"Of course, señor."

"Jose, he's feeding you and the others. We'll meet later."

That chore complete, Slocum in his road-dusted clothing strode in the double doors with the immaculate suit-wearing banker. They crossed the red tile floor and into his majestic office where the two women sipped on wine, crackers and cheese.

"Is that a real buffalo up there?" Pearl asked behind her hand when Slocum came over to see about them.

He checked the wall mounts and agreed. "Grizzly bear, elk and that's a moose."

"You ladies hunt?" Koehn asked.

They both laughed, then grew embarrassed.

"Only for gold, these days," Slocum said. "Only for gold."

"Yes, yes, of course, the gold will need to be smelted into bullion, but I am prepared to cover your expenses until we can arrange all of that."

"Of course. We need ten thousand to send back with the guards. It is half the pledge to the village that helped us."

"I can do that."

"We want a place to stay while the gold is worked."

"I have the finest apartments on the top floor of the Duchess Hotel that will be at your disposal and a chef to cook your meals. Guards under my man, Gregorio, will protect your stay in our city."

"That's good for starters. Tomorrow the ladies will want to see new dresses and we can speak of investments."

"Ah, yes, you will want to make them."

"The ladies are considering a large hacienda."

"Haciendas, yes, I know of several for sale." That time he showed his gold tooth, he smiled so hard.

"Then it has been a hard ride. We need a bath, food and some rest."

"Ladies," Koehn said, sweeping up a glass of wine and toasting them. "To your futures as very rich women."

Slocum wet his sun-crusted lips and smiled. *To eternity, too.*

19

In the distance, a line of saw-edged purple hills touched the azure sky. Slocum stood at the balcony window and felt the morning breeze on his face. Below in the street, the vendors shouted, donkeys brayed and the usual morning sounds of a city street drifted up to him. Magdellania was coming alive. When he glanced over his shoulder, he could see Linda's shapely form and brown skin in a fetal position lying asleep on the great poster bed.

He thought about her *jacal* in the mountains and smiled. Big change for both of them. Bathed, dressed in new silk bathrobes and ready to play the game of the rich. The three had sat up the night before drinking champagne and laughing for hours.

"No more stinking unwashed hinnies to climb on me ever again." Pearl shook the hair from her face. "Stinking bastards, think they are such lovers. Half drunk and half hard. They got a wet noodle they want to stick in you."

Linda laughed and raised the tall glass. "Maybe you will miss them?"

"Miss them, my ass. I will take who I want to bed when I want them. We are very rich, aren't we?"

They both looked hard at Slocum.

"Yes, very rich. When the gold is melted down, you two will be the queens of Magdellania."

Pearl hugged her legs, seated on the floor, and rocked on her butt. "Then we can worry that they are after our money and not our asses." Her laughter rang like a bell.

"What will you do?" Linda asked him.

"Stay for a while. Make sure that you two are safe."

"What if we gave you the money to hire some *pistoleros* and go kill that bastard that murdered Mucho and Tuey?" she asked.

Pearl nodded, leaning forward to hear his reply.

"I plan to go after him anyway."

Linda smiled and shared a sharp nod with Pearl. "But don't leave too soon."

He grinned and winked at them. "No, we need to use this castle a while."

"Since I am the boss—" Linda's brown eyes glistened with mischief. "Tonight you sleep with me."

Whew, what a party. His head still hurt.

At a hiss, Slocum turned and looked across the room. In the far doorway stood Pearl curling her finger at him. The white silk robe opened and showed a seam of brown skin from her buxom cleavage to her black thatch. When he crossed the tile floor, she took his hand, wrinkled her nose toward sleeping Linda's form and led him several doors down the hall.

"So we won't be disturbed," she whispered and closed the door behind them.

Lacy curtains on the open French doors danced in the cool morning air. The great poster bed looked inviting—he had lots of catching up to do on his sleep. She looked up at him, standing before him and unbuttoning his shirt. In response, he toed off his worn-out boots. Then she gripped the waist of his pants and pulled him to her. Her hot mouth began on his chest, kissing him, the quick tongue licking a path down the center of his stomach as she released the buttons on his fly. Soon the room's air swept over his bare butt.

On her knees, she gently molded his scrotum and began to suck on his glans. He wanted to stand on his toes and drew in his breath sharply for control. Then her tongue began to rasp the underside of the head of his dick. His fingers flowed through her hair, then he cupped the back of her head to draw her closer.

Eyes squeezed tight, he savored the pleasure. Her small hand massaging his tender testicles, she worked hard on the business of sucking him off. At last, out of breath, she rose to her feet and led him to the bed.

She dropped the robe on the floor and climbed up on the high goose-down mattress. In the center, she plopped down with her head on the pile of pillows and drew a deep breath.

"Come to me." She veed her thick legs in the air and through her sleepy eyes challenged his advance.

He guided his throbbing dick inside the slick lips. At his entry she cried out, "Yes!"

When he pushed past her restrictive ring, she clutched him. Like the drivers on a locomotive he began to pump forward and back. The swollen walls of her vagina, vicelike, squeezed his pulsating rock-hard shaft. The collar at the front grew even more restrictive and each drive from his butt became harder and harder.

All his effort soon caused a sharp pain in his rectum. A cramp high up inside him began to radiate sharp knifelike strikes each time he went to the bottom of her shaft. Beads of sweat began to lubricate their bellies. Her fingers soon reached underneath and she began to squeeze his balls. Dazzled with pain and need, he felt the rise of his come start up the shaft. Twin needles penetrated both sides of his butt and he drove it home.

She clutched him hard. Threw her head back so far he could glance down and see the ridges of her windpipe in her throat. A roar began deep in her chest and became a scream when his fountain exploded in her. He felt certain she could be heard at some distance.

They lay in a pile, but she made sure when he went down on the bed beside her they were still attached. She scooted in close to keep him in her. Both her hands around his neck, she looked dreamily at him.

"They'd all been like that, I'd never wanted the gold."

He chuckled and bent over to kiss the top of her head. "I thought they were all like that and some were even better."

"Noodles and dog dicks," she said with a shake of her hair. Scooting against him, she used her fingers to part her hair and moved it from her face. "Oh, I could use you all day."

"That would be interesting."

At nine, the salespeople arrived with racks of fancy dresses and undergarments. The two woman became little girls in a candy store. Slocum pulled up a chair to watch. One of the saleswoman started to send Pearl off with a dress to put on.

"He won't watch," Pearl told her and winked at Slocum.

"Oh, my poor dear, you have no undergarments on," the saleswoman said.

"I don't need a corset." Pearl made a face at her.

"Oh, but my dear, it will give you, ah, lift to your bosom."

"You like lift to the bosom?" Pearl asked him with a put-out look on her face.

With a new red dress hooked over her shoulder, Linda hung across Pearl's shoulder and looked hard at him. "He likes lift and the rest, too. Don't you, darling?"

"All of it."

"The tailor's coming for you in an hour," Linda said.

"I don't need—"

Her threating finger waved at him to behave. "You can use some new chaps, canvas pants, a couple of cotton shirts, a new vest and silk scarf."

He sat back and held up both hands in surrender as he watched the brown form of Pearl slip into a bright-blue dress. Too large. She shook her head in disappointment and came out of it. She showed off her naked body to him in a flash, ready to try on the next one. She winked as if to say, I'll be ready for more in a little while.

"Fun, isn't it?"

"Señor?" One of Koehn's guards called to him from the door.

"What does he want?" Linda asked, looking down at the black and white dress she had on.

"I'll go see." He went to the door and stepped into the hall, closing it behind him. The show was for him and not the help. "What's wrong?"

"There is a man downstairs who wants to talk to you, señor."

"His name?"

"Vargas."

That sumbitch had his nerve, showing up in Magdellania after all they'd been through. Slocum stuck his head inside and waited for Linda to cross the room in the stiff green ballroom gown.

Forced to haul the garment up with both hands, she frowned at him. "What's wrong?"

"We have company at the palace."

"Who?"

"Vargas. He wants to talk."

Clutching a dress to her naked form, Pearl rushed over. "What's wrong? You two look serious."

"Vargas is downstairs. He wants to talk." Linda said.

"What does that donkey dick want?"

"Let me guess," Slocum said. "Your money?"

"What if we hire him as a flunky?" Pearl said, obviously amused and pleased with her idea.

"Tell him we are busy now, but will see him at lunchtime," Linda said.

"Your funeral," Slocum said and started to leave.

"No, it will be his if he tries anything," Linda said, so coldly that he nodded in agreement.

Slocum followed the guard downstairs to the lobby.

"Ah, there you are, *mi amigo*," Vargas said and stood, advancing across the lobby. "You tell this hombre I am your amigo, no?"

Looking with disdain at the road-floured man before him, wearing a bandolier cross belt half full of copper cartridges and a week's growth of whiskers, Slocum nodded. "The ladies will see you at lunchtime. Meanwhile, go take a bath. When you return, leave your arms with the guard and bring your manners upstairs."

"Oh, sure, oh, sure, whatever you say, amigo. How are they? The ladies, I mean."

"Mucho and Tuey are dead. Murdered by Cicatrize and his men at St. Tomas two days ago."

"That son of a dog . . ."

"Linda and Pearl are fine. They will meet you at lunch upstairs."

"I'll go take a bath and clean up. Tell them I love them much and am anxious to see them again. You'll tell them, no?"

Slocum nodded to get rid of him. He told the guards the plan and to have him leave his hardware down there. Not that he felt the man might murder them, but unarmed he might be a little less boastful and he could use a whole lot of that.

"What do you think of this dress?" Linda asked, swirling around when he returned.

"Very pretty," he said, eyeing her mounded cleavage, exposed by the low-cut front.

"Not my breasts," she said perturbed.

"Them, too. Oh, I sent him off to take a bath and clean up. Told him to be back at noon for lunch with you two ladies."

"Sounds kinda fancy," Pearl said. "Two ladies, wow. We use to be mountain *putas*."

"I also told him to leave all his guns and ammo downstairs."

"Why is that?" Linda asked.

"To take some of the wind out of his sails."

"He could use lots of that," Pearl agreed.

Linda closed her eyes as if thinking. "It was only yesterday he would come for a swing in my hammock for four ten-centavos pieces."

Pearl cupped her oval chin in her hand. "Now I would ask him fifty pesos for me to do it with him."

"Vargas don't have fifty pesos to his name." Linda shook her head in disbelief at her friend.

"Then he can go jack off." Pearl laughed out loud, making signs like she was doing it with her right hand.

Vargas came all cleaned up and unarmed. He made great bows to both women. A servant took his great sombrero and Pearl took him by the arm into the dining room.

"Bet she's screwing him in one hour," Linda said softly to Slocum as she guided him into the room after them. "She always liked him."

He acknowledged he heard her and held the chair for her to be seated.

"Ah, amigo, this is some place, no?" Vargas said, from across the table to Slocum.

The servant showed him the bottle of wine and Vargas nodded. With a corkscrew the waiter undid the cork and poured a dash into his crystal goblet.

"Oh, no, fill it, hombre." He made signs with his hands.

"You don't wish to sample it, señor?"

"Oh, hell, no, I don't want no sample. I want the whole damn glass full."

Pearl slapped Vargas on the arm. "You are supposed to taste it, dummy."

"How was I to know? I am a poor man."

"You may be all the rest of your life, too," she said sharply.

"I will learn. I learn fast, huh, amigo?"

Slocum nodded. He could hardly wait to hear the man's cock-and-bull story about him running off and leaving them. That would be next.

20

Koehn's man Gregorio mentioned a few names to Slocum. Men he considered as double tough. In his new leather pants, blousy cotton shirt, vest and a straw panama hat, Slocum slipped out of the hotel in midafternoon. He wore squaw boots; the bootmaker would have his new ones made from kidskin in a few days. He also wore a new .45 Colt on his hip. An expert gunsmith was working over his old Navy .44. The revolver spit too much lead sideways due to the gap between the cylinder and the barrel. Also, the man was replacing the main spring that cocked the hammer, the weakest part in the belly gun.

The two men Slocum wanted to talk to were Polo Jiminez and Chako Valdez. The best place, according to Gregorio, to find them was in the Blue Ox Cantina. He took a taxi across town and the man delivered him to the corner where the Blue Ox Cantina's batwing doors in the corner faced the small square. From the size of the testicles on the blue fighting bull's picture, they might have called it *Grande Huevos del Torro*. Amused at his own humor, Slocum paid the taxi man and started for the entrance.

When he pushed open the shuttered batwing door, the aroma of sour booze and cheap perfume filled his nose. A

123

trumpeter began to blast a song about the wild *caballo*. A reckless *puta* began to hat-dance to the music, then she bent over, threw her dress over her back and mooned some grinning hombre seated at a table.

"You like it, no?" she shouted at the potential customer.

"I liked it."

"Good," she shouted, dancing around him with her arms waving like willow limbs over her head. "You like it enough to pay me two pesos for it?"

"I do."

She held out her hand for the money. He raised up in the chair and drew out the coins. Without a look away, he slapped them in her palm. She tossed them to the barkeep, who caught them in both hands and nodded in approval.

"Come on, big man, I want to see that big stick you's got in your pants." She pulled him to his feet and toward the curtained backdoor. Everyone laughing at her words and deeds, they cheered him on.

"You better have an elephant-sized one," some heckler shouted. "Or you'll fall in her cunt and never come out." More laughs.

"What can I do for you, señor?" the bartender asked Slocum.

"They said I could find two hombres here. Jiminez and Valdez."

"Who is calling?"

Slocum turned around and hooked his elbows on the bar to view the rest of the smoke-hazed room. "Tell them that Gregorio sent me."

A hawk-eyed man with a chiseled face came over and stood beside Slocum, sizing him up and down. "My name is Chako Valdez. What you want, señor?"

"Gregorio said you and your partner were tough *pistoleros*."

"Tough enough for what?"

"To bring down a killer called Cicatrize."

"Who is this hombre?" The shorter man frowned his thick eyebrows.

"A killer of women, a raper of little boys."

"Why don't you kill him yourself?"

"I would, but he has some tough hombres that usually ride with him."

"What can you pay?"

"Five hundred apiece to ride out. Another five hundred when he's dead, paid to both of you." Ten times the price most people paid for assassins, but he was buying loyalty, too.

Chako nodded his head that he understood the offer. "Is he in the Madras?"

"Yes, I think so."

"Then you must pay two trackers and my packer a hundred each, whether we get him or not."

"I can do that. I have some good big mules we can use."

"Ah." A smile spread over Chako's dark face. "You work for those rich women who just came to town, no?"

"Yes."

"Tell me, gringo, are they as rich as some say they are?"

"Maybe richer."

"There is a blowhard called Vargas who said he would soon have all the gold."

"They don't pay that much to stablehands. She hired him to look after their animals, for now. Let's have a drink."

Chako clapped him on the arm. "I thought he was blowing in the wind. What do you do for them? Besides kill bastards?"

"Something like that. Can you be ready to ride in two days? I'll have the supplies and the mules ready."

Chako ordered them some mescal. Then he frowned as if thinking. "We'll need two bronco Apaches to track for us. Can I send you word? They are the only ones that can find their own ass up there anyway, unless you can?"

Slocum shook his head, "We'll need them. Send me word at the hotel."

"To our health and his death." Chako raised his glass.

Slocum liked the cold-nerved-sounding man. He clunked his own against Chako's drink. "To his death."

21

When Slocum found Vargas at the stables later, the man was on crutches. "What the hell happened to you?" he asked with a frown.

"That damn Josh mule, he kicked my leg."

"Well, if this job is too much for you—"

"No. No, I'll be fine."

"Good, I want them shod as well as my dun. I want all the pack saddles repaired and the girths in good order or buy new ones."

"For when?" Vargas rested his armpits on the crutches.

"By tomorrow night."

"Tomorrow night?" His eyes widened in disbelief.

"Listen, if this job is too much for you—"

"No, no, I will have them fixed and everything ready."

"Good. There will supplies to receive, also."

"Where are you headed?"

"Hunting," Slocum said and left the man.

"I'd go along!" he shouted.

"Not this time," Slocum said and headed for the hotel across the street.

Something moved in the corner of his eye. In reaction, Slocum dodged behind a water-carrying donkey. A bullet struck the wooden barrel on the far side and water flew over his head. The burro bogged his head and went bucking off down the street, his loud brays shattering the air. Slocum's hand shot for the butt of his Colt and he studied the far side of the street. Screaming women swept up children and pressed for their houses.

Something moved in the corner of his eye. Then gunsmoke mushroomed around a muzzle. Half turned, he answered the shooter with the .45. The shooter dropped his gun and grabbed for his arm, then he was gone behind some food stands and Slocum was running after him.

The gunman wasn't Cicatrize. This one had a mustache and Slocum didn't recall seeing him before. He held the pistol high and people fell aside to let him through. The high-crowned hat disappeared around a corner and Slocum slowed down, wondering about an ambush. He ducked into a dry goods store and raced down the aisle for the backdoor. Maybe he could head the shooter off.

"I need out back there," he shouted at a man busy sorting clothes.

"*Sí,* señor. The door is open."

"*Gracias,*" he said and ran past the storekeeper.

In the alley, he looked both ways, seeing nothing but refuse. He ran to the left to where the other alley intersected. Halfway up the refuse-strewn way at the side of the dry goods store wall, he saw a man collapsed on his butt.

"You work for Cicatrize?" Slocum demanded, seeing the man was unarmed. Must have dropped his pistol.

"Huh?" The man blinked in the too bright sun at the sight of him, holding his bleeding arm with his good hand.

"How much did Cicatrize pay you to kill me?"

"I don't know who you are, señor."

Slocum drew out a large bowie knife and used the tip underneath his chin to raise his face up. "This help your memory?"

"Five hundred in gold."

No doubt gold from the Ray robbery. Slocum whirled at the sound of footfalls coming toward him. He relaxed at the sight of two of Gregorio's guards with rifles.

"We heard shooting, señor," the older one said.

"*Gracias.* Turn this *pistolero* over to the police."

"Get up!" the younger guard said and not so gently jerked him to his feet.

"The señoritas were worried about you," the older one said.

"Thanks," Slocum said and they headed up the alley for the street.

"Where is that bastard Cicatrize now?" Slocum asked the prisoner.

"I don't know, señor. I swear on my mother's grave, I only met him last night."

"Where?"

"Cantina Olivos."

"It is in the barrio. A tough place," the older guard said.

"I'll remember that." Slocum nodded to the two guards and hurried across the street. They could handle the law. He was anxious to report to the two about his new hirees and plans.

"You all right, amigo?" Vargas shouted from the door of the livery on his crutches.

Slocum waved away his concern and hurried through the traffic. As if that worthless bastard even cared. He glanced up and saw Pearl searching the street from the balcony. She smiled big when she spotted him, waved and turned to go inside.

He crossed the lobby and bounded up the staircase. On the second flight, someone stuck a pistol out from the flight above and fired at him. The shot deafened him and the gunsmoke boiled out in the stairwell. Slocum drew his .45 and made ten more steps, looking out of his watery eyes for any sign. He could hear boots going up. He doubled his effort and took them two at a time. On the second floor, he managed to get a fleeting shot at someone's coattails going into a room.

He rushed down the hall into the room and saw the open window. Standing in the wind-swirled curtains, he spotted three men on horseback fleeing up the alleyway. Had his ambush been a trick to draw off the guards? He wondered if the women were all right. Holstering his six-gun, he raced upstairs and, out of breath, collapsed with his shoulder against the wall at the sight of the two blanched-faced women coming out of the apartment.

"You're all right?"

"Yes. But we heard more shots?" Linda said.

They each took an arm and guided him inside. "What happened? We sent the guards to help you."

"That's what they wanted. I think they were on their way up here to get you."

"Where did they go?"

"Jumped out the window into a cart in the alley and they rode away."

"Was it him?" Linda asked.

"Damned if I know, but who else dislikes you two? Hell, I only caught a glimpse of them."

"What now?" Pearl asked, looking up and down the hall, then closing the door and bolting it.

"Guards stay here, no matter what. We double them. I'm going after Cicatrize with the two men Gregorio mentioned. I met one and he's tough. They'll do to ride with. Chako, the one I met, is getting two bronco Apache trackers."

"What if Cicatrize still is in Magdellania?"

"I'm sending word for those two to meet me tonight in the barrio. We may not need pack animals after all, if he's here."

"What is Valdez doing?" Linda asked, looking out the open French doors.

"Him I have working. Oh, a mule kicked him and he's on crutches."

"Too bad it wasn't his head," Linda said and motioned to indicate that Pearl was coming back with champagne and glasses.

Slocum smiled and winked at her. He shared her opinion about the man.

22

Chako Valdez and his man Polo Jiminez sent back word they'd met Slocum at a water well in south Magdellania. The square was set in a small area under a few cotton-woods and palm trees. Even this late at night, some bare-breasted women still washed clothes in the troughs set for them to use. They laughed and gossiped. With his shoulder leaned against the tree trunk, Slocum waited and whittled on some stringy cottonwood in the bloody twilight that filled the square.

Some half-grown children teased a young pig by keep-ing it from heading for the ditch that the sudsy water ran into. The long-snouted barrow squealed and tried to bluff them, but they used switches to turn him back each time he attempted to run by them. Impatient with his tormentors, he squealed even louder. His commitment only brought laughter from the boys and girls. As they cavorted with the pig, it became obvious the girls in the crowd wore no un-derwear under their too-short dresses.

"Señor?" Valdez said, joining him. "This is Polo."

Slocum nodded and started to put away the knife in a sheath behind his back. The irritated pig at that moment made a real charge, rooting children aside and running through one of the boys' legs. The shouting rider managed to stay on the pig's back for a few seconds, then he spilled off into the dust. Everyone laughed at him, including the washer women. A toothless one with flat, flabby tits ordered one of the young girls to come help her.

"What do you need?" Chako asked Slocum, when they found him.

"Cicatrize hired a man to ambush me this afternoon after I met with you and then he tried to enter the hotel where the women are. The *pistolero* I shot told me he met him only last night down here at the Cantina Olivos."

"A tough place, but we can check it for him. Tell us again what this Cicatrize hombre looks like."

"A bad scar down his left cheek. They say his head is shaved."

"Cicatrize. You ever hear of him?" Chako said to his taller partner, who in the fading light looked like the handsome one of the pair.

"I only heard of him," Polo said with a head shake, then he smiled at Slocum. "You are the one with the rich women I heard so much about. Where did you meet them?"

"In the mountains and—" Slocum began his story as they walked in the shadows close to the buildings. Much of the plaster was gone off them and some looked deserted; others had candle lamps lighted in them. Children in the doorways asked them sharp questions when they passed them. The three ignored them and the hard-looking *putas* who spoke of their expertise at making love for only ten centavos. Women, too old, too ugly, too fat, too diseased or on too many drugs to work uptown.

"And this mine, you know where it is?" Polo asked, sounding impressed.

"Yes, but I fear more earthquakes have buried it."

"Why is that?" Chako asked.

"Why wouldn't Cicatrize be working a rich, unguarded

gold mine, instead of risking getting his ass shot off down here?"

Chako bobbed his head in agreement. "Because it is all caved in?"

"Exactly what I think. In an hour, you could hand pick out a fortune from the vein I saw up there," Slocum said as they drew up in the shadows and Polo pointed out the Olivos across the street.

Slocum could hear the music and laughter of the *putas*. Drunks staggered in and out of the open door. A yellow light defused by all the smoke shone out the entrance on the rock sidewalk. Horses, burros and mules were hitched at the rack. Most looked asleep, standing hipshot in the pearly starlight.

"I can ask the questions," Chako said and gave a toss of his head.

"Fine with me," Slocum said and they started to cross the street.

"There is a man called Franco runs the place. He is a tough sumbitch," Polo said and Chako agreed with a nod.

"Your game," Slocum said. "I want Cicatrize and the bulldog-faced one works for him."

"If they're here, we'll get them."

"Good enough."

The thick smoke in the barroom formed a hazy yellow light under the candles set on wagon wheels overhead. Bearded tough-eyed men followed their entry, chewing and smoking on cigars. Others sat in drunken stupors with their mouths dropped open and slobber running out.

One hungry customer suckled like a starving man on the bare tit of a *puta* seated on the table before him. The hardcases around him sloshed the beers out of their mugs and cheered him on.

Chako led them to an open space at the bar and ordered drinks. When Slocum reached for the money to pay, Polo stopped him. "Our treat."

"Fine, but I ain't seen a sign of the two we need in here."

"We'll know in a few minutes if they've been here and where they went."

"Oh, Polo, what brings you here?" The one asking was a swaggering kid hardly out of his teens. His shirtsleeves were too long and swallowed the hand holding the schooner. Wild fuzz grew on his chin.

Polo spoke sharply to him. "We're here looking for a bulldog-faced guy."

"You mean Tauber?" The boy cut his narrow-eyed glance around to be certain no one else heard him.

"He work for Cicatrize?"

The boy, acting sober, nodded and then finished off his beer.

"Where's he at?"

"He was here last night." The kid set his mug on the bar.

"Where is he at now?" Polo asked.

"I heard they left this afternoon." The kid acted anxious to move on.

Before he could step away, Polo caught him by a fistful of the shirt, jerked him around and gave him a swift knee to the crotch that drew a groan from the kid. Never wavering, Polo drew him close to his face.

"Listen and listen good—that's half of what I'm giving you if you ain't got the answers for me," Polo said in his ear.

Coughing hard and holding himself with one hand, the kid looked ready to cry. "—there was a *puta* on Verde Street."

"What's her name, you little prick?" Polo insisted.

"Melania." The kid choked some more and had to put his hand on the bar to steady himself. "Tauber liked her."

"Melania who?"

"Melania Riley, I think."

"Where on Verde Street?"

"Near the Oso Negro Cantina."

"You see this scar-faced one in here?" Polo finally let go of his shirt.

The kid snuffed up his nose and nodded. "Last night."

"Where did he go?"

"I heard the mountains."

"How many men does he have working for him?"

With a bland look at them, the kid shrugged. "How should I know?"

Polo scowled at him and the kid relented, holding his hands out. "I don't know, honest to God. I swear to the Virgin Mary. I don't know this guy."

"Pay him two pesos," Polo said and turned to his beer on the bar like the kid never existed.

Slocum dug them out of his vest pocket and paid the boy. Then he watched him hustle himself out the front door. Satisfied his help was damn sure tough enough, Slocum turned back to his own beer and looked at the nude over the back bar. Gaudy and out-of-proportion, she was not appealing to him. He shook his head. "Guess we learned all we can here?"

"Tauber may still be in town," Chako offered and sipped his beer. "We can go over there next."

Slocum agreed. They finished their schooners and left the bar.

An hour later, a bartender in a sleazy dive sent them up an alley to Melania Riley's *jacal*. The quarter moon was up and bright. At the sight of a short mountain horse standing hipshot in the shadowy light, Slocum held out his hand.

"His horse?" Chako whispered.

"Can't tell, but he's the kind they ride up there."

"I'll cover the backdoor." His gun in hand, Polo slipped between the hovel two doors back from hers and went off in the night.

"You want pussy?" asked a potbellied woman who came to her doorway with a roll-your-own hanging in her lips.

Chako stepped to her. In a stage whisper, he growled,

jerking her by the arm close to him. "I have a peso. Answer me right and you get it. Make a fuss, I'll cut your throat."

"No fuss."

"Is the bulldog-faced one in there with her tonight?"

The frightened whore nodded frantically and Chako let her go. Slocum paid the woman. Then the two men split. Slocum went wide left, Chako went right and they closed on the front door. There was a light on inside the hovel, and Slocum could see two silhouettes on the blanket over the door.

Chako nodded to Slocum, then he stepped in and drew the blanket back with his gun barrel.

"Don't move a muscle," the *pistolero* ordered.

Gunfire broke out. Chako jumped back and Slocum's shoulder hit the wall, his six-gun cocked and ready. All he could hear was her screaming. Then there was some scrambling in the *jacal*. He shared a nod with Chako. Tauber was getting away out the other side through a window.

More shots. Slocum figured they must be from the outlaw and Polo. When they rounded the *jacal*, Slocum was in the lead and saw a bare-headed man seated on the ground.

"Polo's been shot. See about him," Slocum said to Chako and headed down the alley after the retreating Tauber.

In the moonlight, Slocum could see that all the man wore was perhaps some short pants. Running as hard as he could in the soft-soled squaw boots, Slocum worried the outlaw was outdistancing him. Tauber was headed down a dry wash and attracting several cur dogs on his heels.

Out of breath, Slocum slid to a halt and raised the pistol. "Stop!" When the outlaw never slackened his stride, he fired and Tauber went facedown. Gasping hard for more air and halfway bent over, Slocum tried to recover his breathing and holstered the gun. He must have really shot the killer. No movement in the prone body that he could detect in the starlight slugging up the loose sand. He hissed away the dogs, after one mongrel went over, hiked his leg and pissed on the still body.

At the sound of someone behind him, Slocum whirled, drawing his Colt and ready.

"You get him?" Chako asked, coming off the bank.

Putting his gun away, Slocum nodded. "He ain't moved since he fell down. How's Polo?"

"He'll be fine. Not serious, but we will need him doctored." Chako squatted on his boot heels near the outlaw's head and nodded at Slocum on the other side, then spoke to the prone man. "You dead, hombre?"

Then without a word, he grasped a handful of Tauber's hair, jerked his head up and stuck a knife to his throat. "I don't think you are dead, *mi amigo*."

Tauber let out a cry of panic. Chako bent over him, holding the knife hard enough to the outlaw's throat that dark blood began to seep onto the bright blade.

"Where is the scar-faced one?" he hissed through his teeth.

"I don't know."

"You got two seconds to remember." He pulled the man's head up higher by the fistful of hair and forced the knife's keen edge deeper into the side of his throat. The process drew more cries from Tauber.

Then at last, the outlaw shouted, "Valley of the Moons. He's got a camp there. Let me go!"

In one swift slice, Chako slit Tauber's throat from ear to ear and cut off the outlaw's screaming. He dropped the head facedown in the sand and the outlaw's legs thrashed their last. Wiping the blade on his britches, he matter-of-factly nodded to Slocum. "Let's go get Polo seen about. You ever been to the Valley of the Moons, hombre?"

"Once, but an Apache led me in there."

"Apache's going to lead us there this time, too."

"We can take Polo to the hotel. The girls will be pleased to know Tauber is dead." Slocum looked off in the darkness at a yapping cur. Be many days' ride to get up there, too.

23

"Tuey's killer is really dead?" Linda asked Slocum with a scowl written on her face.

The doctor was in the next room looking at the extent of Polo's wound. Chako nodded his head for her, walking the floor and beating his high-crown sombrero on his leg.

"The doctor can fix him," she said to the short man who actually was about the same height as her.

"Oh, he is a tough hombre. He's been shot before."

Slocum brought a bottle of mescal and some glasses and motioned to the couch. "Have a seat. We can't do nothing. That sawbones got to do it."

"Oh, señor—" Chako looked around as if distressed by the place.

"Sit down," Slocum insisted. "That's what they rent this room for."

Linda interceded and took his hat. Standing in front of him, she used her other hand to straighten the stubborn lock of hair over his eye.

"*Mi amigo,* I owe you so much for killing that bastard." Toe to toe with the *pistolero*, they looked into each other's eyes.

With a head shake and a grin, Slocum poured mescal

into the glasses set on the table as if he had no idea what was happening.

"I don't feel right being in such a fancy place," Chako apologized to her.

Slocum picked up his drink and watched her fingering his shirt as if straightening it. Neither moved away, still toe to toe.

"What can I do to make you more comfortable?" Linda asked in a husky voice.

"*Caramba*, woman! You are stealing my brains."

"Good, that is what I want to do. You work for me, don't you?"

"If you say so . . ."

"Come then," she said and took him by the hand. "Excuse us," she said to Slocum with a twinkle and led the shell-shocked Chako away to the bedroom. "We have work to do," she said over her shoulder, disappearing from the room.

Slocum toasted them and finished his drink. The Doc and Pearl came from another bedroom into the main part.

"How is Polo?" Slocum asked.

"He's going to be fine," Pearl said smugly. "The bullet went through and he's going to be well soon. Right, Doc?"

"Yes, he's healthy enough. Be fine in a day or so with Pearl's good care." The doc accepted the glass that Slocum offered him. "He's lucky to have such a wonderful nurse."

Pearl beamed, taking a seat on the other couch.

His drink down, Doc nodded in approval. "I better be going to making my rounds, getting to be daylight out there."

She sprung to her feet and showed him out, asking all the time about what she should do for the patient. In a minute she returned.

"Where are the others?" Pearl asked.

"In bed." Slocum indicated the closed door.

"Already? They didn't even wait for the doctor's report."

"I don't think they're sleeping, if that's what you mean."

Pearl touched her forehead and shook her head. "I'd better go in the other room and see about Polo. He may need something."

"Wild horses couldn't keep you out of there," Slocum teased. Then when she stopped as if to be with him, he waved her on, laughing. She made a face at him and stalked away.

He yawned and stretched his arms over his head. Damn *pistoleros* had stolen his women. Amused, he went to the first empty bedroom and flung himself on top of the bed; sleep would be fine for him. Polo still needed to be well enough to ride to the mountains. He closed his eyes, thinking about Chako pounding it to Linda's fine butt—my, my.

"We better leave Polo here to watch the girls," Chako said with Linda hanging on to his shoulder.

"That's fine with me. You get your Apaches and packer. I'll have the stableman, Vargas, get the mules ready." With his gun arm in a sling, Chako's partner had no business up there.

"In the morning, we leave," Chako said, patting her hand and looking up at her.

"You must be careful, my cherry."

"Careful! I am always careful."

Slocum rose from the table. "Do I need to tell Valdez anything else?"

"No," Linda said and turned back to fuss over Chako.

Slocum found the stableman taking a nap. He cleared his throat until Vargas bolted up and blinked at him. "What do you need?"

"A hour before daylight, I want the mules loaded with the supplies. Is my dun reshod?"

"Oh, *sí,* señor. Can I go along?"

"No, you watch things here."

"*Sí,* amigo. I can handle things for you."

What could he handle? Slocum had no idea. But he could handle something. Actually Vargas's days might be numbered even as a stableboy; Pearl had taken a shine to the good-looking Polo. Besides, the man was going to recuperate in their suite of rooms and guard them. If Vargas was still working there when they returned from the Madras, Slocum figured on being surprised.

The coolness of predawn invaded his shirt and vest. Paul, their packer, was charging about, sending Vargas hither and yon for things. In the deep shadow, squatted in their knee boots, two men with bronze skin and hatchet-sharp features observed all with the eyes of hawks. No mistaking them— bronco Apaches in once-white cotton loincloths. Silver concha belts around their waists and eagle feathers woven into their bobbed black hair, with blue headbands. Both Apaches wore loose-fitting collarless blouses the ash-tan color of the soil. Across their knees rested new oily-looking Winchesters.

Chako took him over to them. "You can call him Fly."

The younger Apache acknowledged the word when Chako said it and nodded to Slocum. The other one was older, fuller-faced and thicker-built than Fly.

"His name is Booty."

Slocum nodded, knowing not all Indians liked to shake hands.

"Him big bossman," Chako said to them, indicating Slocum. In return they nodded to both men.

"Unless you have a better idea, I want to camp tonight at Polo's cousin's ranch. Paul can bring the mules and catch up with us there."

Slocum agreed and he went by to check on Paul. The packer knew where to meet them, so Slocum forked the dun horse full of feed and found him spunky enough he was forced to check him. A grin in the corner of his mouth, he realized that the pony might unload him if he bucked hard enough. Unwilling to allow him any slack, he jerked a few times on the reins to keep the dun's head up as they rode down the side streets of Magdellania so as not to make themselves such a big target.

Slocum, Chako and the two Apache trackers trotted their horses. The drum of their hooves echoed in a clapping sound off the adobe buildings and hovels. Strings of vendors with loaded burros were entering the city.

"What do you know about this hombre, Cicatrize?" Chako asked, riding stirrup to stirrup beside him.

"Not a lot. They say the Comanches gelded him years ago. They supposedly gave him the scar, too. The women think he is part spirit and can change forms."

"What do you think?"

"I think he's a mean sumbitch. Anyone who would murder a beautiful woman like Mucho in cold blood is no good. And I think he ordered that butcher Tauber to garrote Tuey, another lovely woman."

"The spirit part?"

Slocum shook his head to dismiss the man's concern. "He may not have balls, but the rest of him is real."

The man threw his head back and laughed. "No *huevos*."

24

They reached Polo's cousin's *ranchería* in late afternoon.
The man's attractive wife came running from the house at
the sight of Chako, then halted when she obviously did not
see Polo with them.

"Where is Polo?" she asked.

"Aw, he had small accident," Chako said, dismounting
and hugging her. "He ran into a bullet. Only a scratch.
Don't worry, little one, he will be fine. Dorita, meet my patron, Slocum."

She used her hand to shade the slanting sun from her
face and smiled at him. "Good to meet you. Get down. Any
friend of Chako's is welcome here."

"Thank you, ma'am."

The Apaches took both of their horses with their own to
water and the two of them followed her to a remada. She
dipped them out a drink and passed around the gourd
dipper.

"Polo is all right?" she asked Slocum.

He smiled at the dark-eyed beauty with her pointed
breasts that jiggled under the blouse and shapely body.
"Yes, he is guarding my bosses."

"Oh, are they important men, your bosses?"

"No, they are beautiful, rich women."

"No wonder he had to stay there and recover." With a wide, knowing smile, she shook her head, making the silky waves of her hair roll on her shoulders.

"Where is your husband, Benito?" Chako asked, looking around.

"Gathering some steers to sell. A man wanted to buy some to make oxen. He is supposed to be coming to get them in a few days. I expect him by sundown."

Satisfied with her answer, Chako nodded and handed her back the gourd for a refill. "Paul is coming with the mules later." He stretched his arms over his head and yawned. "Perhaps a siesta would be nice now."

"There are hammocks over in that shade." She pointed to the next one nearby to them. "I will cook a goat—maybe two for such a crowd to feed."

"She can cook wonderful goat," Chako bragged.

"I bet she can," Slocum agreed, watching the turn of her hip as she hung the gourd up.

"Some shut-eye, *mi amigo?*"

"Fine." Slocum never refused a chance to sleep when the opportunity offered itself, He'd missed lots of shut-eye in his time and would no doubt miss some more on this mission before it was over. Stretched out in the hammock, hat over his eyes, he drifted off.

Something awoke him. The bloody light of sundown flooded everything when he raised his hat. He caught sight of the youngest Apache, Fly.

A quick look around revealed nothing. "What's wrong?"

"Horse comes back. Blood on the saddle."

Slocum threw his leg over the side of the hammock and scrubbed his sleepy face with his calloused hands. He twisted around to see that Chako was still asleep.

"We better wake him. Chako! Get up!" he hissed.

"What!" The man bolted up.

"Hush. A horse came in just now with blood on the saddle." Slocum did not want to panic Dorita. The animal might not be her husband's at all.

"Oh, whose is it?"

"We don't know. Fly said he just came in."

"If anything happened to his cousin Benito, Polo will be angry." Chako rose and knifed in his shirttail.

Slocum pulled on his new boots. Once his feet were in them, they reminded him how new they were. Strapping on his gunbelt, he followed the Apaches and Chako through the mesquite brush to the corral.

"That's Benito's buckskin. Where's Booty?" Chako looked around for the second Apache.

"Gone to backtrack him," Fly said.

"Good thinking. I better go and tell her." His look filled with dread, Chako stared at the ground. "You want to go with them, Slocum?"

"Of course. You handle the woman. It may turn out all right."

"I hope so."

Slocum tossed his saddle on the dun and led him out of the corral. Chako had already gone back to tell her and when he mounted he heard Dorita's screams of protest coming from the direction of the casa. Better Chako than him having to handle the distraught wife. He set his heels to the dun and hurried up the sandy dry wash after Fly's mustang.

The greasewood flats spanned toward some low hills. Fly led the way and Slocum trusted the youth with reading the signs Booty left him. After his few of years of experience with General Crooks' men, Slocum learned the Apache scout's ability to follow a track.

They entered a canyon of black volcanic origin and the narrow trail clung to the side of the steep cliff. In the twilight, the sound of their horse hooves on the hard rock echoed back. At last, they reached a pass and paused to rest their horses. The rising night wind swept their faces. Still no sign of Booty or Benito. With a nod for him to lead, Slocum reined the dun in after Fly and they went off the far side.

A mile or so further, Fly held up his hand to stop them. He pointed to the north. There was a flare of match.

"Answer him," Fly said.

Slocum struck a match that made a bright enough flame to make him blink.

"There!" Fly pointed at another flash. "He saw it. He's up ahead."

They trotted their ponies in the duller light. Not familiar with the land, it was bisected with some deep washes, any one of which could cause an unsuspecting headlong plunge ten to twenty feet into the bottom.

When they reached Booty, he was kneeling beside a prone body. Slocum dismounted and dropped the reins.

"How bad is he hurt?" he asked, squatting down beside the Apache.

"Him no talk."

Slocum felt for his pulse on his neck. Faint, but there was a small one. He tried to see in the night what had happened to the man.

"Hold a match up," he said to Booty as he got on his knees.

When he rolled the body over, he saw the blood in the match's flare. Shot in the back. But by who and why? Benito had lain there for some time, too. Lots of the blood was already dry.

"Did they rob him?" Slocum asked letting him back down.

"Dorita—" Benito managed. "Protect my Dor—"

"Don't worry about her. Chako's looking after her. Who did this to you?"

"I didn't—know him. Cattle buyer . . ."

"He have a name?"

Benito put his hand to his cheek. "Bad scar."

"We've got to get you home. It won't be easy."

"Whatever. . . ."

Slocum looked around the starlit desert. Nothing to make a stretcher out of for miles. "We'll have to hold him in the saddle."

Booty nodded.

Slocum knew one thing. The ride back might kill the young rancher. But he'd for sure die out there. He'd already lost lots of blood and, jarred around on the way, back he might lose even more. Maybe he should try to bind him up. Nothing he could think of would serve as a wrap.

"Hey, it's going to hurt, loading and riding, but we're taking you back to her."

"I don't know you, but God bless you—"

He could be introduced later. The biggest thing he wanted was to get him back to the ranch and that would be painstakingly slow on a walking horse.

With Slocum holding him in the saddle at last, they started back for the ranch. Benito repeatedly went faint and it was all Slocum could do to hold him on the horse. The distance back to the foothills proved lengthy. Then, on the narrow trail, Slocum thought he had lost him. But they eventually made it off the mountain and were on the flats.

Fly rode ahead to tell Chako to send for some medical help. Benito's blood had soaked onto Slocum's new shirt and pants. The loss worried him, but there was nothing he could think to do but hold him in the saddle and push on. Both arms around the slender form, he managed to keep him on board until they drew in the lights of the ranch house.

"I sent a boy for the doctor," Chako said, rushing out with Dorita crying and wailing on his heels.

"Oh, my Benito, are you all right?" she cried, wringing her hands.

"He's unconscious. But he's alive," Slocum said as they eased him off his horse.

"Who did this?" Chako asked under his breath as the two Apaches carried him to the remada.

"Our man Cicatrize. You seen him around here?" Slocum surveyed the place in the starlight.

Chako frowned. "No. He supposed to be here?"

"Benito was worried about it."

They carried Benito's slender form into the *jacal* and put him on a pallet. His wife washed his face and knelt beside him, moaning and pleading for him to live. In between doing that she raised her eyes to the ceiling and besieged the Virgin Mary to intervene.

Slocum was more concerned about the wound in his back, but wondered if a doctor was coming. He turned and asked Chako.

"There is a woman that helps sick people," Chako said. "They have gone for her."

Slocum nodded that he had heard the man. A medicine woman might not be enough for his needs. Nothing he could do for the moment but fret. And where was his ghost, Cicatrize?

The sharp blast of a Winchester outside sent his hand for his gun butt. Then another report. He and Chako rushed to the open doorway.

"What's happening?" Chako asked Booty, who was outside holding his smoking rifle.

"Someone was sneaking up here." The Apache waved at the dark mesquite brush.

"Get him?"

The Indian shrugged. "Who knows."

Who knows. The notion turned over and over in Slocum's mind. Was the ghostlike killer out there?

25

Spirits leave no tracks. In the predawn, Booty squatted in the dust with Slocum; the Apache showed him the prints of whoever he had shot at in the night. They obviously had managed to escape back toward a dry wash.

Slocum drew a heady snootful of the creosote bushes that perfumed the desert and rose. "Follow his tracks. I'll get our horses. You and I need to see where he went."

The solemn-faced Booty agreed and set out.

Back at the corral, Fly caught Booty's Indian pony for Slocum. The second thing on Slocum's mind was the fact that the packer, Paul, had never shown up the night before, either. Earlier, he'd discussed the packer's no-show with Chako, who admitted it was strange for his dependable man not to have been there. But shorthanded, Slocum decided for Chako and Fly to guard the ranch while he and the other scout went searching for the mysterious night visitor.

The medicine woman had done what she could to staunch the flow of Benito's blood, but Slocum was convinced that if the bullet didn't come out the poor man's chances were not good. Filled with concern about the whole deal, he short loped the dun to the dry wash and handed Booty the reins to his roan.

"There were three here." In a bound, the Apache was in the saddle and they headed east.

Three men in total. The Winchester-bearing scout and he could handle that many if push came to shove in this deal. He wanted to sink his teeth into Cicatrize, not bad enough to blunder into his lap, but bad enough. The picture of Mucho's ripe body pale and cold made his guts threaten to erupt. They loped toward the sun and the mother mountains still beyond the horizon.

At midday they came to a village. Slocum wanted to water their horses and get some food. Booty pointed out that the tracks of three went into the cluster of scattered *jacals* around some palm trees and obviously a well.

"Keep your eyes out for them," he said to his scout as they walked their horses toward the well area. How did Cicatrize put him and Benito together? Somehow he felt the move on the young man was planned. Chewing on his lower lip, he squinted against the bright sun and undid the rawhide loop over the six-gun's hammer.

There were two carts in the square hitched to oxen. The men loitering around were not locals. The one dressed in brown was a gringo and he acted asleep, slouched on a bench, but Slocum caught him sneaking a peek at him and Booty. Another who wore a red sash around his girth with lots of black whiskers was leaned against one of the cart wagons. The third man whittled, looked up at them blandly and whittled some more. Slocum dropped heavy from the saddle. Using the dun for a shield, he pulled down the crotch of his pants and nodded slightly at Booty.

"Nice morning," the brown clothed man said, lifting the brim of his hat with his thumb.

"A good morning," Slocum said, letting the horse drink.

"You and that red nigger up here on business?"

"Guess if I was that would be my business." Slocum met the man's glare. "You making it yours?"

He rose and flexed his arm. He wore a fingerless glove on his gun hand.

"I ain't had the pleasure of your name?" Slocum said. The whittler still held the knife in his hand and Whiskers was on Booty's side.

"Rafter, Rafter Kims."

"Slocum's mine."

"I heard of you. Folks say you're fast with a gun." Kims pulled his glove on tighter and made a smile that didn't go to his cold hazel eyes.

"Tell me. You work for Cicatrize?"

"Never heard of him."

Kims' answer came too fast. The *pistolero* wasn't there to simply challenge Slocum to a gunfight.

"How much is he paying you?"

"Mister, I come to kill you—" Kims' hand shot for his gun butt, but the roar of Booty's Winchester distracted him a second too long. Slocum's renewed Navy .44 spoke death from the muzzle and the lead projectile sent Kims staggering backward. Pivoting on his heel, Slocum swung the Colt around and blasted the whittler with his six-gun half out. The man, hit solid in the chest, doubled over.

Smoking gun in his hand, Slocum kicked the whittler's pistol across the ground and kept his eye on Kims' form, sprawled on his back. When he reached the gunfighter and looked down in his blanched face, he saw the blank look of death begin to cloud Kims' eyes.

"Where in the hell is Cicatrize?" Slocum shouted aloud. Then he pivoted on his heel to go where the Apache squatted beside the bearded one.

"Where is he?"

"I'm . . . dying, for christsake." The big man held his guts with the blood seeping through his fingers and brighter than the red sash.

"Mister, you came to kill or be killed. I want answers or

I'm turning this Apache loose on you. You won't last long, but it will be worse than hell, what he can do."

Slocum checked around; the townspeople were still too afraid to come out and show their faces. He was aware that the whole gunfight thing might have been to engage him for a sneak attack.

"Where was he to meet you?"

The man's eyes half-closed and he shook his head.

"Cut off his dick first," Slocum said to Booty. Glancing around, Slocum felt anxious to get on, and the skin was crawling on the back of his neck over his concern that they still were in a trap.

When the Apache whipped out a butcher knife and took one step toward him, Whiskers screamed, "All right, he's gone to the mountains for more gold."

"What for?"

"How should I know?"

"What did you do to the pack train?"

"We shot the packer and the mules." Whiskers shook his face and winced at the pain.

"When did you see Cicatrize last?"

"Two days ago . . . Magdellania."

"How did he know about the mules?"

Whiskers shook his head.

"Why did the three of you stop at Benito's ranch last night?"

"To see if we could kill you. He . . . said you'd be there."

Slocum drew a sharp breath up his nose. "How in the hell did you three know we would be there at that ranch?"

"He told us—" Whiskers slumped over and died.

"Who did he say told them?" he asked Booty.

The Apache shook his head warily. He'd never heard it, either.

Slocum punched the spent casings out of his pistol and reloaded it. A spy in their midst and he had no idea who it could be. Was it one of the guards? Who knew that much about their business? Damned if he could think of anyone besides Chako and Polo that knew anything about their plans and the packer, Paul, worked for them. No sense to it.

For a long while, Slocum considered what to do next. They had no supplies; they were no doubt rotting where they shot the mules and Paul. The ride to the mountains was several days across the desert. No matter how badly he wanted to revenge Mucho's and Tuey's death—he needed to take some common sense into account.

"We better go back to the ranch," he said to Booty.

The Apache agreed with a nod.

"I'll go find someone and have them bury the bodies for their horses, guns and clothing."

Booty followed along and they went inside the cantina. Slocum bought a bottle of mescal and they both drank a couple of shots from it. The bartender agreed to have them buried and divide the spoils. That matter settled, the two rode back to the ranch.

26

Past midnight, they returned to Benito's. Fly was on guard and met them in the darkness at the edge of the mesquite and greasewood.

"Everyone is here. Paul and the pack train were slaughtered."

"We learned that. Who is here?" Slocum asked as he dismounted heavily.

"Polo, the two women, a man from the stables—"

"That would be Vargas."

"*Sí*. They sent that boy that works for Benito for a doctor from Magdellania." The youth looked them over in the starlight. "You did not find Cicatrize?"

"No, only three of his hands who wanted to die."

"Where is he?"

"The dying one said in the mountains to get more gold." Slocum shook his head warily.

"At the mine?"

"If it is still there. Or his camp, where he might have had some gold left that he stole off a man called Ray."

"The woman Linda asks about you."

Slocum smiled and clapped the youth on the shoulder. "The novelty of Chako may have worn off."

Fly shook his head as if he did not know.

For the moment, Slocum wanted some sleep. He sent Booty off with his horse and told him to get some shut-eye, too. When he reached the ramadas, Chako met him.

"You didn't find him?"

"No, only three of his hired guns. I spoke to Fly coming in. Sorry to hear about Paul, but his killers are in hell."

"*Gracias*. He was a loyal man."

"I want you to think about the spy in the middle of us. Those three knew we were stopping here last night. Save for Booty's shooting and running them off we might all have been dead."

"I'd cut this spy's ears off if I found him," Chako said.

"Me, too. First we have to find him."

"Slocum?" A sleepy husky voice in the night came toward him. Linda, wrapped in a flannel blanket, came over to see him in the rising moonlight. "You all right?"

She hugged him tight. "I'm so sorry about these messes I get you into."

"No worry, but right now I need some sleep." He shook his dull head to try and clear it as he hugged her.

"Come, mine is still warm." She led him to her hammock.

In minutes, with her ripe body tucked under his wing, he was asleep in the swing and dreaming about Cicatrize.

He couldn't see the outlaw's face for a shadow. But the man taunted him from his place high on a wall.

"So you have shot my men and now you are mine. For me to shoot you."

The gun in Cicatrize's hand exploded over and over again. Gunsmoke obscured the shooter. Still no bullets hit Slocum's body. He flinched each time the outlaw shot. Was he that bad of a shot or was he shooting blanks to scare him? Slocum sat up, wide awake, in the teetering hammock and cold sweat ran down his face.

"What is wrong?" she whispered.

"I've been having nightmares."

"So sorry." And she pulled him down on top of her. Her fingers fought with his pants and soon they were off his hips. Deftly, she played with his rising erection, spreading her legs apart and easing the head of his dick into her gates.

His hips ached to hunch it to her hard as he gently punched his growing sword inside her. A soft "ah" escaped her lips as he entered her turgid ring of fire and she clung to him. Soon they both became involved in the hard forces of reaching pleasure's heights. The walls began to expand and closed around him, tightening their grasp and rubbing his tender dick hard. The pleasure in his brain grew greater and greater. These zephyrs were taking him to new mountain peaks that staggered him into such a dizziness that he feared he would totter and fall any minute. Yet they continued.

His raucous breathing and her dreamy moans were audible enough he figured they would wake everyone. Then something slammed him across the butt with a post and needles struck both testicles. He made his final drive deep into her. She arched her back for the fountain of sparks that flew from his swollen dick into her.

Out of breath, they collapsed and he fell asleep. No dreams.

The five men squatted in the dust by the corral for a conference. Polo's bandaged arm was in a sling. Chako was looking still vexed over the spy deal and the two Apaches showed little concern for anything.

"First, we have no pack train," Slocum said, thinking out loud.

"To ride up there and look for him will take some supplies," Polo said and acted taken aback over the loss of the train and Paul.

"We can't go without them," Slocum said. "Best we send back and get some."

"Don't let the spy know our plans." Chako shook his head again over the matter.

"I won't, unless it's one of us."

"Makes you wonder," Chako said.

"How's Benito this morning?" Slocum asked, looking at them for an answer.

"The doctor says he has a chance," Polo said.

"Good. One of you go for the supplies; take an Apache along. Meanwhile the other scout and I will head for the mountains. We can meet you up there. I'm sure we can scrounge up enough to eat around here until you get there."

"Who will watch the ranch?" Polo asked.

"You and the girls. They can shoot straight," Slocum said.

He agreed with a nod.

Slocum rose and looked around for Vargas. He had not seen him yet that morning. "Where's Vargas? He can shoot a gun."

"He's still asleep," Chako said in disgust.

"I didn't say he was super help."

Everyone, even the Apaches, laughed.

They decided that Booty was the most experienced scout, so he and Slocum rode out before noon for the mountains. Linda kissed him good-bye with concern and told him to be careful.

They rode through the village of San Tomas and the bartender in the cantina told them no others had come by. The dead men were planted and their goods divided. Satisfied, Slocum and Booty went outside, mounted up and rode on.

That evening they camped at a spring the scout knew about. Slocum was grateful, but he was aware the Apaches had knowledge of all this desert. Watering holes that white men rode past without even seeing could suffice an Indian and his horse. After a silent meal of beef jerky, they rolled up in their blankets and slept a few hours.

Long before dawn, they hit the saddles and were mountain bound. After sunup, Slocum's sand-pit-feeling eyes watched the dust devils dance over the flats. In late afternoon, they stopped at a natural tank and bathed in their clothing to cool off and to spend the night. They could see the Madras peaks in the distance when the sunset shone on them.

Slocum hoped for some word about the outlaw in the village they'd make the next day, a place he had carefully avoided with the gold train. Valdez was a village that traded with bronco Apaches and outlaws that hid in the Madras. That was how they existed—by illegal trading with outlaws. Residents were not the most savory; still, if Cicatrize had been there, someone had seen him. And for a small price would tell on him.

Valdez sat at the base of the foothills where a stream called the Oro came from the mountains to irrigate a few fields. Some cottonwoods lined the stream banks. The main small fields of corn and beans were fed by water diverted from it.

Brown children in tattered rags romped and screamed. Busy playing with a pair of burros, they only took dark-eyed snapshots at the two when they rode up through the *jacals* to the town's only cantina.

Dismounting in front of the place, Slocum did some knee bends to loosen himself up. With no sign of any hostiles, he motioned for Booty they'd go on inside.

"Good afternoon, amigos," the bartender said and grinned big as if expecting someone with real money had entered his establishment.

"Bring a bottle," Slocum said.

The man was quick to take one off the back bar and put it with two glasses on the counter. "Anything else, señor?"

"We're looking for man called Cicatrize. Has he been in here lately?"

"No. No. I don't know that one." The man backed up holding his hands up defensively.

"How much do I owe you?" Slocum scowled at the shorter man.

"Three pesos."

Seated at the side table, Slocum shook his head at Booty. "We must be chasing a ghost." He blew out his breath in exasperation.

"No ghost. Him leave tracks."

"You been seeing them coming up here?" He pushed the glass across to the scout. "Then you're better than I am."

Both men laughed and then downed their mescal. Of course, he expected the Apache was a better tracker. Slocum looked around the dingy, dusty barroom and wondered what he'd do stuck in a place like this forever. With his palm, he drove the cork home and nodded to Booty.

"Time we got after him."

The scout agreed.

"Oh, señor, don't leave so soon," the bartender said. "I just sent for some lovely girls to entertain you."

"Next time, my friend. We've got to find your friend Cicatrize."

"Oh!" the bartender wailed. "Please don't mention my name to that one."

"Lots of folks feel that way." Slocum carried the bottle in his left hand and pushed his way out into the daylight. Something was wrong. No sounds of the kids shouting— he turned an ear to listen.

The bullet chipped a cloud of dust from the mud plaster. Slocum ducked down, drawing his Colt and searching for the shooter.

"Where's he at?" Slocum asked the scout at the side of his horse with his Winchester ready. The small puff of smoke, he thought, came from the roof of a house on the hill.

Booty shook his head. "Him over there someplace." The Apache indicated the *jacals* on the rise to the northeast of them.

"You circle behind. I'll cover you."

Booty set out in a run. Nothing popped up. No shooter.

The Apache reached the cover of some mesquites with several other hovels blocking him. Then Slocum heard the drum of a horse galloping away.

"He's gone!" he shouted to the scout.

Holstering his gun, he shook his head. The ghost had escaped again. Though he felt certain it wasn't the real one who'd shot at him. There was little doubt in his mind that Cicatrize would not have missed him at that range.

"Maybe we can catch him?" Booty shoved the rifle in his scabbard.

"Maybe we can be ambushed, too. He knows we're coming after him. So we lose the element of surprise." Slocum stared at the distant Sierra Madras swathed in purple. "We let him wait."

A questioning frown crossed Booty's dark face.

"Let him worry about where we are for a while."

The Apache nodded and smiled when he brandished the bottle of mescal. "Thank God, I didn't break it. Let's go meet these pretty girls he's got coming."

Cicatrize, two can play cat-and-mouse games.

27

With his calloused hand, Slocum rubbed his palm over his whisker-bristled mouth. From the small window he could see the first pink peeps of dawn. A rooster crowed half-heartedly. Maybe if he had not been up all night with those two pullets, drinking rotgut liquor, maybe his head wouldn't hurt as bad as it did.

On the bed, the shapely brown leg and hip that stuck out of the rumpled covers belonged to the *puta* called Mia. That part of her exposed in the shadowy light of the room, the sound of her soft breathing was in his ear. Booty had already gone for their horses. The other girl, Rita, was making coffee. The strong aroma of it filled his nose. Earlier, he'd given her the money to go buy some. He tossed some pesos with a clink into the bed with Mia. Quickly, she clutched them in her fist, never opened her eyes and in a sleepy-sounding mumble managed, *"Gracias."*

In the main room, Rita kneeled at the fireplace. When he came in she turned and smiled, reaching for the pot to pour him some coffee. He took the steaming mug and squatted down.

"This man we seek, Cicatrize. Does he come here often?"

She shook her head. A mestizo girl in her teens, her

163

brown eyes conveyed the wisdom of a much older person. "And everyone is grateful he comes so seldom here. He hurts people when he comes. He likes to hurt people."

"Little people who can't fight back."

"Yes. Little people and they think he is a ghost. They wake up and he is in their bed, holding a knife on the man's throat and raping his wife."

The coffee tasted rich—he nodded his approval. Booty returned and joined him and she poured him a cup. Soon she served them plates of scrambled eggs, peppers and sausage with tortillas and plenty of red sauce on the side. When they finished, he paid her and they rode on.

"There is another way into the mountains. So they could not ambush us," Booty said as they rode. "Apaches used it."

"Good. Can you leave a sign so the others can find us with the supplies?"

The scout bobbed his head that he could.

"Show me the way, my friend."

At midday leading the dun, on foot, up the narrow canyon's confines, he mopped the back of his neck with his kerchief. The place was an oven with no wind. He looked ahead uphill and there was no end to the house-sized boulders or the crease in the sky that the towering cliffs formed. All he knew at this point was that the Apache ahead of him knew the way—he hoped.

Booty stopped at a trickle of a spring that formed a small basin, then quickly disappeared into the ground. The cool water revived Slocum some and he glanced skyward.

"We be on top soon," Booty promised and set out in his knee-high, pointy-toed boots, leading the roan.

It couldn't come soon enough for Slocum.

An hour later, the fresh wind swept his sweat-soaked face and he smiled. They rested, man and beast in the pass. Ahead he could see the rolling hills of juniper that led to the main mountains. But the trail looked open enough to ride through and he was grateful to have the canyon passage over at last.

"Where is the Valley of the Moon?"

"Bad place."

Slocum turned and frowned. His scout had never acted superstitious before. Where were they headed?

"What's wrong?"

"Smells bad. Lots of stinking water."

"Hot springs, huh?"

"Bad breath of the spirits there."

"You know where his place is there?"

Booty nodded his head and prepared to mount up. "We find him."

That was right. They would find him. Coming in the back way might help if Cicatrize expected him to come in the front door. Left boot toe in the stirrup, Slocum bounced off his right foot and sprung into the saddle.

"Can we go in there from the back side?"

"That's the way we go." Booty twisted in the saddle and nodded at him.

They rode for an hour and Slocum was relaxing in the saddle as the sun climbed. His scout held up his hand and motioned for them to go to the cover of some tall junipers. Once there, Booty held his roan so he didn't whistle to the stream of horses and riders going by in the swale underneath them. Slocum did the same to the dun.

"Broncos," Booty said.

Slocum nodded, grateful his man had not let them ride into them. Women and children rode double on mountain ponies; some had three riders. Their possessions were piled on a travois that scraped on the ground like a hissing snake. Men with red headbands and spanking their war ponies with brass-tack-decorated rifles herded the camp southward.

"You know them?"

Booty nodded. "This band calls their chief Spider. He

never went in with Geronimo. People say he is a son of Who."

He acknowledged the scout's words. Who was the notorious war chief of the southern branch of the Chiricahua Apaches who died, some said, of a heart attack. By Slocum's count there were about a dozen women of child-bearing age in the group. Maybe two dozen children from toddlers to teens. The men were harder to count. They rode on the flank and some were no doubt out ahead of this precious train. He was looking at the last of a handful of broncos that had not been annihilated or captured and sent off to slavery by the Mexican authorities.

They waited until there were no longer any sounds of the movers. Then they mounted up and headed to the northeast—away from the broncos. By midafternoon the way grew rougher and outcroppings of black lava flow began to appear. Booty pointed out they needed to cross one more range, then they'd be in the Valley of the Moon. He failed to say being a billy goat would have helped.

The narrow trail up the sheer face of rock convinced Slocum his dun horse was good. One misstep and they'd fall to their sure death. The side of his new boot scraped the rock wall on the left side and the other hung out over nothing but blue sky. When he glanced over the side, he looked down on turkey buzzards floating up on currents far below.

The dun finally scrambled on top of a flat perch and Slocum mopped his wet face despite the cool wind. The way ahead was troughed out from there and, while steep, it led into a grove of spindly pines that looked like a small park where they could dismount and rest.

"We're there." Booty led him over to the edge to look down. Black outcropping marked the valley, along with the rising vapors from the various steaming hot springs.

"Where's his place?"

"In the far end."

Slocum nodded, considering all the things that had passed since he'd found Ray on the road, shot in the back. It had been a while. The image of poor Mucho and Tuey haunted him. He owed Cicatrize a share of what he'd dished out.

He and Booty gnawed on some spicy beef jerky, washed it down with tepid canteen water and rested until sundown. Then they jerked their cinches tight and remounted for their ride through hell. Slocum checked the loads in his Colt as the bloody sky sank into a gathering curtain of blackness. In a few hours, win or lose, this thing between him and the ghost would be over. One would win, one would lose.

He smelled the brimstone brewing long before they reached the bubbling caldron. The plopping of the mud added to the sounds of crickets and locusts.

"Plenty bad place," Booty said, riding in close.

"I agree. How far to his place?"

"Maybe a few miles."

"Good." He booted the suspicious dun around another smelly pool.

The last mile, they left their horses in a grove of pines and went on foot. His scout led the way on the side of the mountain. A quarter moon was up and Slocum could make out some corrals and the outline of log buildings. He could smell wood smoke in the air. A few lights from lamps shone.

"Any sentries?" Slocum squatted on his heels and they surveyed the camp.

"He keeps some on the entrance." Booty used his arm to motion to the north.

"How many are here?"

Booty shook his head. "No way to know."

"You come in from the left. I'll circle in from the right and we'll start taking them out."

The Apache nodded and moved out in the night. A dog

began to bark and someone silenced it with cusswords. Both men froze. Then only the night insects' chorus filled the canyon and a few voices talking in Spanish carried to them. Slocum nodded to his man and they moved again.

He reached the back of the log cabin and listened. Some man was arguing with a woman inside. The shouting match reached a high pitch. Then Slocum could hear him slapping the woman and her moaning. In minutes the man stormed outdoors cursing her out loud. Slocum could hear his footfalls coming around the house. He eased to the corner and when the man came by him he hit him over the head with his pistol. Knees buckled, the man went down, groaned and Slocum applied another blow that silenced him.

He took the man's handgun and knife—and left him there. He moved to the next cabin. Someone inside was snoring. With light steps he eased himself around to the open front door. On the front stoop a log flooring creaked when he stepped on it. The sleeper stopped breathing. Slocum, gun in hand, held his breath and froze. Long seconds ticked by, the man gasped then went back to snoring. Relieved, Slocum slipped into the sour-smelling room. A bad odor of dirty feet and booze filled his nostrils. He made certain only one was asleep in the room.

Beside the bed, he jammed the pistol in the man's face. "One false move and you go to hell."

"Huh? Huh?" The man tried to sit up, then wide-eyed looked at the muzzle of the Colt. "What you want?"

"Cicatrize."

"Huh?"

"Hush or you're dead. Get on your belly."

"All right. All right. I don't know where he is."

"That's all right. I'll find him." Slocum used the man's suspenders to tie his hands behind his back. Then he tore a strip off the blanket and made a gag around his mouth. Next he used the man's belt to tie his feet; that complete, he straightened.

"You make a sound, I'll come back and slit your throat. Savvy?"

"Mmmm."

A hatless figure stood in the doorway and Slocum reached for his Colt. Then he saw the rifle and realized it was his man.

"Any sign of him?"

Booty shook his head, then looking around from the doorway. "There are a few men playing cards in one cabin up the way."

"This one don't know where he's at. He says anyway."

"Should we take the men?"

"I guess, and cover our backsides so he don't slip up on us." Slocum was looking over the silver area between them and the pens. Beyond the corrals, tall pines shaded the mountainside into an inky black.

"Where's the dogs?"

The Apache drew his hand across his throat to indicate he'd taken care of them.

Slocum nodded. What had to be done, had to be done. The two headed for the card game, staying close in the shadows of the buildings and looking in all directions for any sign or threat.

The Colt's redwood grips felt wet in his palm, despite the cool night air. When they drew near the shaft of light spilling into the yard from the open doorway, he could make out the voices of the men making small talk.

Slocum eased himself beside the small window and peeked inside. Four men at the table. Two women in low-cut dresses stood watching the game. He drew back and took a breath. Holding up four fingers, he nodded to the Apache for an answer.

The scout answered with a nod he was ready. Guns cocked, they both stepped inside.

"Don't anyone move! Hands high or die." Slocum knew if one shot was fired in the room, the results would douse the flickering candle flames. Then in the ensuing darkness, there would be lots of wild shooting. He held his breath and jerked the handgun from the nearest outlaw. All four were standing and the wide-eyed women, too. He tossed knives and guns aside moving to his left—his gun ready. Booty worked the opposite side.

"Where's Cicatrize?"

No answer.

"Everyone against the wall over there." His gun barrel for a guide, he ordered all six of the muttering crew against the walls. To clear things, he sent the table crashing over; cards and money flew aside. His fierce action caused the half dozen to look wide-eyed at the two guns.

"This man's an Apache." Slocum indicated Booty. "He's going to notch one of your ears to start with unless you tell me where Cicatrize is—"

Then he heard the damn taunting laughter. He and Booty exchanged hard looks. The understandable drum of a hard-racing horse going away came next.

"The son of a bitch has given us the slip again." Slocum gritted his teeth. Maybe he was a ghost.

28

Before they left his hideout, they set fire to all of his buildings and supplies. Then, leaving the disarmed outlaws only
a few burros to ride, they took the herd of horses and mules
and headed up the mountain trail. All the firearms of any
value that weren't tossed in the fires were loaded on a gray
mule along with the ammo.

Aside from the small amount of money on the men,
there was no sign of any gold trove. Slocum couldn't find
out anything from the gang members either, though he
doubted the head outlaw had told them anything about his
stash, out of fear they'd help themselves.

From the top of the pass, Slocum could look back and
see the smoke boiling up. He'd need to rebuild his hideout,
too. For certain, the downtrodden outlaws were too lazy to
fight any blaze. Well started on fire before they left them,
the cabins would burn to ashes and the gang members
would make their grueling way out on burros and foot.

"Which way did he go?" Slocum asked Booty, who was
on the ground assessing the tracks.

"North."

"Maybe toward the mine," he spoke his thoughts out
loud. Cicatrize heading in that direction perplexed him.

Perhaps he had treasure hidden in the area. No telling.

Leading the loaded gray mule, he began to gather the loose animals from their grazing and send them up the valley. Booty swung on his roan and helped him. Once the herd was moving he sent the scout ahead to look for signs.

"Be careful. He'll try to trick us and ambush us."

The Apache agreed and sent his horse around the herd. He soon disappeared down the wide valley. Slocum was left to loose-herd them. They moved out at a trot and churned up dust. He wanted them far enough away that the left-behind bandits couldn't catch and use them.

At midday, he let them drink at a stream coming off the mountain. He'd dismounted and pulled his pants away from his crotch when he had the feeling he was being watched. With the dun for his cover, his right hand eased for his gun grip as he pivoted around studying the timber line for sight of anyone.

Then he followed the curious looks from the horses and spotted them. Three hatless riders on horseback in the shadowy light under the pines to his right. Broncos. He wet his chapped lips and wondered. Did they know his business? Had they seen Booty when he went through? For ten cents he'd give them the whole herd. Then he'd be certain the ponies didn't ever get in the wrong hands.

How should he communicate with them? Then there was the gray mule with the arms. Had they seen the rifles sticking out of the packs? Hard to miss. Mexicans could charge him with gunrunning if they found out. Though he didn't give a damn about Mexican officials anyway. Some well-connected merchant would sell them arms and ammo and get by with it.

One thing to do—go see what they wanted. He holstered the Colt, used his knife to slice off a small pine sapling. The sticky bark on his palm, he stripped off the few boughs and then tied a white kerchief on the end, all the time looking up occasionally at the threesome. They made no hostile moves.

Satisfied they were waiting for this strange-acting white man, he made it into the saddle on the second try. He caught up the reins and settled his toes in the stirrup, found his seat and, bearing his flag of truce, started for the three broncos.

The one in the middle was older. He wore a ragged army shirt, open in the front showing the wrinkles on his brown belly. He squinted like someone nearsighted. As Slocum got closer, he saw the red skullcap he wore and the rifle over his lap. The other two were bare-chested young men balancing rifles on their legs,

Slocum halted the dun at a hundred or so feet from them. He nodded. "You Spider?"

The chief nodded and the three laughed. The buck on the right had to circle his anxious pony back in place. Gold coins on a rawhide string around his neck glinted in the filtered sunlight. They looked hawkeyed at Slocum.

"You know Cicatrize?" he asked them.

"Them his horses?" Spider said and indicated the dozen or so head grazing behind Slocum's back.

"They are. I want him dead."

The three broncos nodded in agreement.

"I would pay those horses for him dead."

Spider raised up his head and straightened his broad shoulders. The expression never changed. "Hard to kill a *bruja*."

"He is no witch."

"You leave us the mule, too. We will try."

The other two nodded in agreement with him.

"Big price to pay. Many horses, fat mules," Slocum said, acting undecided.

"Leave the gray one, too," Spider reminded him.

"I will. One of us will get him." He took the kerchief off the flag and tossed the stick down.

"What they call you?" Spider asked.

"Slocum."

The Apache nodded as if satisfied.

Ready to leave despite his apprehensions over his own welfare, Slocum turned the dun and started to ride off. He wondered if any minute there would be an ear-shattering war cry and a hot bullet would strike his back. The dun soon hit a short lope and Slocum rode wide of the curious horse herd that lifted their heads to look at his departure. Finally, beyond their rifle range, he eased some in the saddle. He might have made a good trade. Besides being rid of the herd, this gave him a chance to catch up with Booty.

Midday, the Apache scout rode out of the timber and headed him off. "You turn them loose?"

"No, I traded them for Cicatrize."

"To who?"

"The broncos."

"They stop you?" Concern spread over his brown face.

"Nope." Then he told the story of his trade.

"You're plenty lucky." Booty acted impressed. "Wonder why they didn't kill you, then take the horses."

"They hate him, too. Besides we didn't need all those horses. I think Spider was weighing his chances. He can't risk losing many more men in battle."

"Him smart old man." Booty made a serious bob of his head to confirm it.

"We still on his tracks?"

Booty nodded. "Better wait. Pack train comes." He indicated to the west.

While Slocum couldn't see or hear them, he knew they must be—his scout said so. Maybe make a fire and they could have a cup of coffee when the supplies arrived. His teeth were about ready float out for some. He took the mescal bottle from his saddlebags and tossed it to the Apache.

"Lets have a drink. We've got him on the run. More help's on the way."

Booty grinned. "Gawdamn good deal." He popped the cork and took a deep draught from the neck. Wiping his mouth on the back of his hand, he laughed. "Maybe they got better firewater, too."

He handed the bottle back and circled his horse around. Slocum was still looking to the west for sign of them. "Wouldn't be hard if they have any at all."

Fly rode in first and dismounted. Slocum shook his extended hand.

"No Cicatrize?" the younger Apache asked, looking around.

"He got away. Booty, tell him about our deal. I need to get this fire going."

Slocum went after more dry wood. He carried an armload back down hill when the others rode in.

"You all right?" Linda asked, riding over.

"I'm all in one piece. Where's Pearl?" He dropped his wood.

"Hanging back." She shook her head and dismounted, coming over to hug him. "Her and Polo are making love, I guess, back there."

"Nothing wrong with that."

She swept the long black hair from her face and smiled. "No, I guess not. I was worried about you. Did you get him."

He hugged her tight, feeling her hard nipples against his chest. "No, but we disbanded his gang, put them afoot and burned his camp."

"Where is he?"

"He may have gone back to the mine."

"I thought—"

"The next earthquake covered it. So did I. But we can't be certain until we go back and look. He may be there."

She squeezed him tighter and buried her face in his shirt. "I'm so glad you are safe."

It went the same for him. He laid his cheek on the top of her head and rocked her in his arms. Glad to be safe, but Cicatrize's haunting laughter still niggled him. He looked at the peaks above them and the azure sky—*I'll get you yet.*

29

He squatted in the pass, joined by both scouts. The midday sun glinted off the mica in the boulders. "What did you find?"

"He maybe at cabin." Booty gave a toss of his head.

"The cabin is still there?"

"Yes, many slides around it." The older scout used both hands to show him the flow of landslides from three directions. Fly backed his demonstration.

"Plenty bad place."

Slocum rubbed his upper lip on the side of his hand. The whisker stubble itched. That could mean Cicatrize was in the shaft getting gold out or trying to. "You all stay here. I'll go down there and if he's there I'll settle with him."

"I'm going along, too," Linda said, hurrying downhill.

"No way. These mountains are liable to slide off any minute and bury anyone down there."

"You can't stop me."

He considered her defiant stance. Hands on her hips. Dark eyes glaring at him. He shook his head in defeat, looking at the two Apaches for counsel.

"Women warriors are the toughest," Booty said and grinned.

"Get your horse then," Slocum said and scowled after her.

"What should we do?" Chako asked.

"Keep everyone up here safe. We'll be back—one day—I hope."

"Be careful, amigo."

"Why is she going?" Pearl demanded, riding up to them on her horse.

"'Cause she's hardheaded. You stay here 'cause someone needs to spend all that money." Slocum finally laughed. Everyone wanted to go and no one even should be considering it under the conditions, including himself.

"There's some water," Chako said, hanging a few canteens on his horn. Polo was checking the chamber on his rifle to be certain it was loaded to the gate.

"I'll get you another riata," Fly said and ran off for it.

"Why does she want go down there?" Vargas asked, leering over the edge.

Slocum shook his head. The dumb guy couldn't even see the real canyon, it was further over.

"She's got more money now than she can spend," Vargas grumbled.

"Ask her," Slocum said, seeing her returning wearing a bandolier of cartridges crisscross over her breasts and a man's peaked sombrero.

"I'm ready."

"I can see you are. Let's ride." He stepped into the stirrup and swung his leather pants leg over the dun. "Everyone wait here a day for us."

"I will ride a ways with you," Booty said and Slocum agreed; seeing she was mounted, he set out down the trail.

The rocks, talus and dirt carried a yellowish hue. The trail was a narrow steep one that descended down into the bench of pines far below. Slocum leaned back in the saddle and let the dun have his head. Half an hour later they emerged from the stand of pines and took a ledge that went to the next rise. If one fell off the side that his boot hung over; there was nothing to stop him for thousands of feet. He glanced back. Linda rode between them on a good sorrel mountain pony. She forced a smile, though he could tell the deep drop off had her thinking, too.

Slocum looked ahead to where they would again be back in the security of some timber, perhaps a quarter mile further. To have this open space crossed would make him feel better. A handy place for an ambush like Cicatrize used the last time, closer to the cabin. When the dun struck the loose ground on the far side and had to cat-hop up the hillside, Slocum dried his palms on his pants.

They rested their horses in the singing pines. Wind through the boughs made its own song. He handed her a canteen. In gratitude, she smiled, with perspiration running down her face, making dark streaks in the dust. Watered, they booted their mounts on.

They were dropping off a steep hillside when the dun spooked and planted all his hooves. He slid a few feet and stopped.

Linda gave short scream. "What—what's wrong?"

"More aftershock, I guess." Slocum noticed the vibration and let the horse set in place until he settled down. He also heard more rumbling like a good-sized landslide somewhere around them.

"Look." She pointed to a rimrock over them. Tons of rock slid off the plate in a huge avalanche. Slocum held the spooked dun in check until the house-sized rocks rested in a cloud of dust, sending rivulets of smaller ones rolling down the hillside.

Linda forced her horse to get aside the dun. Looking warily at the rim line above her, she shook her head. "Reckon it's smart to go on?"

"No," Slocum said.

"I-I don't want to go back—but when will it do that again?"

"Any minute or two days from now."

"This is not a good idea."

"Fine, you and Booty ride back."

"It ain't going to happen that way." She shook her head, still looking distressed. "You go back with us."

He shook his head. "I'm going to find Cicatrize."

"Then—" She compressed her lips and fire danced in her dark eyes. "You lead the gawdamn way."

"Yes, ma'am."

"And don't yes, ma'am, me."

He pushed the dun on.

Past noon they stopped and overlooked the mine canyon. The massive landslides had changed the looks of the surrounding sides. Giant ponderosa pine trunks stuck out of great beds of freshly loosened rocks. Others had been splintered to toothpicks, boughs tore off them like weeds hoed away. On the ledge halfway down the far side, the roof of the cabin could still be seen caught in a massive river of large rock. Far below, the slides had dammed the main canyon and a lake was beginning to form.

The effects of Mother Nature left them silent in their observations. No sign of anyone or a horse. But even at the distance, using Slocum's telescope, there was nothing, but the chimney and the shingle roof in view from their vantage point.

"How do we get over there?"

"We sure can't take the horses over those slides," Slocum said.

"Guess we walk then," she said and dismounted.

"Going over those boulders won't be waltzing in a ballroom. You can stay here and wait."

She laughed aloud, then she shook her head in disbelief at him. "I never danced in a ballroom in my life. Remember, I'm the *puta* from Sierra Estria."

"Hell, you're the patron now." Slocum winked at the Apache.

He nodded in agreement.

"You going, too?" Slocum asked the Apache when he dismounted.

"Better go see how she makes it."

"All right, you two. What do we take over there?" she asked.

"Our ropes. A couple of canteens and a rifle or two. Stuff some jerky in your pocket. The café over there ain't much good."

"What else?"

"Wear some gloves. Those fresh cracked rocks will be sharp as knives."

She unrolled a pair of man's pants and began to wiggle into them under her skirt. "What are you looking at? I came to go with you."

A big grin on his face. "Hell, I'm just enjoying the scenery."

When she had the britches up to her hips, she bent over, threw up her dress tail and mooned him with her shapely brown butt. "There, you can see it all."

Slocum began to chuckle, then he and Booty laughed until they about cried.

She worked down her skirt and fluffed like an angry hen, but could hardly suppress her own amusement.

Using his tongue to dislodge a piece of jerky in his teeth, Slocum set out with a lariat slung over his shoulder and a rifle in his right hand. She took the canteens and Booty took the other riata and his own rifle.

The slide filled the head of the canyon with freshly broken-off-looking boulders. Slocum gave her hand up and they skipped over the flat to the tilted tops for a hundred feet, then the going grew harder. He hoisted himself on top of a large one, then he pulled her up while Booty scooted around on the knife-sharp edges and met them on the other side.

In front of them was a two-hundred-feet-wide fill of loose cherty rock and dirt. The least-stable looking section and the steepest-faced part so far was ahead of them. Booty started across and his left leg hit a soft spot. Facedown, he found himself spread out and sliding downhill inch by inch as Slocum and she watched.

"What should we do?" she hissed.

Slocum had the lariat undone and ready to toss. Booty found a toehold and stopped his descent. Still spread over the ground and holding his rifle in both hands over his head, his position was precarious.

Uphill or down, Slocum was trying to make up his mind where they could cross over the loose section—much looser than it looked, even, and once one went to sliding it wouldn't end till the bottom some fifteen hundred feet below.

"Go easy."

Booty nodded he heard him. He tried a new toehold with his right foot. The move was slow and calculated in inches.

"Should you throw him the lariat?" she asked.

"I miss and he moves, it's down the canyon."

Stern-faced, she nodded in agreement.

The Apache tried to dig the rifle into the loose material. It only gave way. Slocum watched small rocks begin to come loose under the scout's boots. They wouldn't hold for long.

"Forget the gun. You need to catch this rope." Slocum prepared to toss it, stomping the rocks underneath him to be certain they would hold when the shock of Booty's weight hit the end of the lariat. She moved in behind him and took hold of the rope.

"Forget the gun," Slocum repeated, concerned the Indian might not want to give up the new weapon if there was chance he could save it. He twirled it over his head and tossed it. At the last minute, Booty raised his arms and, as the loop went over them, Slocum jerked the slack to tighten the noose.

Booty began to slide away. Then faster.

Linda screamed, then she set back with Slocum on the rope. In a cloud of dirt, the scout flew downhill, making an arc to their left. Then, with them braced, he came scrambling up the rope with his rifle in hand.

Slocum, Linda and he collapsed on the ground and fought for their breath. Too close to call and they were a long ways from being across. Shaking their heads in disgust, they sat in defeat. It would take a day to go around, if they could even get there then with all the new slides.

"Look," Booty said. "Isn't that a ledge sticking out up there?"

Slocum looked and nodded. "But we'd be out on an eagle's roost when we got over there on the far side."

"Let ourselves down with the ropes."

Slocum turned to her. "Maybe you should go back?"

"Not on your life."

So much for that idea.

Their climb over the rocks up the face took thirty minutes. The edge looked secure enough and they moved slowlike, being certain their feet had a firm place before they moved to another. At last they were on the point and Slocum looked down and gauged the distance. Both lariats combined should let them down. He tied them together, then put the loop around her under her arm. So it wouldn't cinch up on her, he made a knot she would have to loosen to escape once on the next level.

"It looks solid enough," he said, peering off the side. "But you move across it for those trees. Don't stop for anything."

"You are coming?"

"Yes, Booty and I'll be there in a few minutes. I hate to leave the rope, but we may need to swing out of here anyway." He securely tied the tail to the exposed trunk of a pine tree buried in the debris, then went to the lip and took hold of it as she let herself over the rim.

"See you," she said with confidence.

The slap of the bullet sent dust in his eyes. Standing exposed to the world, she dangled in midair on the rope he held standing in the open on the rimrock. The *wang* of the bullet came next. Booty moved beside him and frantically looking down the sights of his rifle at the puff of smoke in the pines downhill.

Slocum fed the rope out hand over hand. "See him?
"No."

Then the cackling maniacal laughter filled the canyon. *He had them right where he wanted them.*

30

Linda hit the deck and quickly fought the rope over her head. She looked up and Slocum gave her a wave to run for the trees. Booty motioned for him to go down. The second bullet hit the rocks and spit bullet fragments in Slocum's face.

This time Booty sent lead in the direction of the smoke. On his knees, Slocum backed off the rimrock with the rope in hand. They were committed and, win or lose, they were going down.

"We can lower the rifles on the rope," he said and down the rope he went. Hand over hand with his feet wrapped in the lariat, braking his descent. He dropped to the ground and looked up for Booty to take the rope up for the guns.

The scout looked over the edge at him, nodded and drew it up. Soon his Winchester came down. Slocum untied it and signaled to take the rope back. He scanned the area where the shots came from. Nothing.

Cicatrize had new plans—if he only knew them. He could see her standing in the shelter of the pines, looking anxious for him to get over there. Booty's rifle came next and the scout also descended the rope from over his head.

Slocum clapped the Apache on the shoulder and they

185

headed in long strides over the last of the slide to the woods. Once there, they caught their breath.

"Where's he at?" she asked.

"Somewhere down there toward the cabin I would say. Maybe one of Booty's bullets found him."

"We could hope so."

The Apache nodded and set out through the trees. Slocum didn't have time to stop him. He and Linda rushed after him, taking some care to check on things around them. They found Booty squatted near the site of the shooter's position.

In his fingers, he held up a copper cartridge. "Him long gone."

"On foot?"

"No, got horse." He pointed in disgust off to the south.

Slocum hugged her shoulder. "He knows the mountains better than we do. Looks like he got away again."

"Shall we try to get some more gold out?" Linda asked.

Slocum nodded, then he looked at the pine-clad slopes above them. He'd get him. Someday, somehow.

A month later, Slocum sat on the veranda of Linda's newly purchased casa. The sun was setting and the night insects sizzled. He saw three riders filter through the twilight, cross the stream and come toward the house. His first thought was to go inside and get his sidearm. None of them wore hats. He held his place.

The middle one spurred his pony and gave a coyotelike yip as he drove up to the porch. He drove a lance in the ground that bent under the weight of some object on the end of it.

"*Gracias,* amigo" he shouted in Spanish, then yipping like a coyote he rode off to join the others, already riding away in the starlight.

"My heavens, what is going on—" Linda stopped in the lighted doorway.

Slocum had vaulted over the rail and was there to examine his gift. He scratched a match and it ignited. In the blaze, he could make out the bald head that looked out of shriveled eyes and the large scar down the cheek.

"What is it?" she asked, leaning over the porch, hugging her arms and trying to see in the gathering darkness.

"We've got paid for some horses. The broncos brought us Cicatrize on a stick."

Watch for

SLOCUM AND THE PRESIDIO PHANTOMS

318th novel in the exciting SLOCUM series

from Jove

Coming in August!